*Titles by Loren D. Estleman*

THE WOLFER
THE STRANGLERS
BLOODY SEASON
THIS OLD BILL
MISTER ST. JOHN
THE HIDER

# THE WOLFER

*Loren D. Estleman*

JOVE BOOKS, NEW YORK

This is a work of fiction. Names, characters, places, and incidents are either the product of the author's imagination or are used fictitiously, and any resemblance to actual persons, living or dead, business establishments, events or locales is entirely coincidental.

THE WOLFER

A Jove Book / published by arrangement with
the author

PRINTING HISTORY
Previously published by Pocket Books
Jove edition / December 1999

The Penguin Putnam Inc. World Wide Web site address is
http://www.penguinputnam.com

ISBN: 0-515-12704-3

A JOVE BOOK®
Jove Books are published by The Berkley Publishing Group,
a division of Penguin Putnam Inc.,
375 Hudson Street, New York, New York 10014.
JOVE and the "J" design
are trademarks belonging to Penguin Putnam Inc.

PRINTED IN THE UNITED STATES OF AMERICA

10   9   8   7   6   5   4   3   2   1

*To John Wayne*
*(1907–1979)*
*In Memory*
*Feo, fuerte y formal*

*A wolf*
*I considered myself*

　　—Santee Sioux song

# THE WOLFER

# ONE

R. G. Fulwider hated winter, which in his view was another good reason why he shouldn't have been where
he was.

It was early March, and back in New York the sun would
be warm on the pavement and attractive women would be
bicycling through Central Park in culottes and starched
white blouses and flowered bonnets, heads held high while
they pretended ignorance of the admiring looks they drew
from male passersby. But along this stretch of the recently
completed Northern Pacific Railroad it was still winter, and
to remind himself of that depressing fact he had only to
rub the frost off his window and glower out at the treeless,
snowswept terrain of northern Dakota Territory hunkering
under a sky the color of mildew.

He was grateful for two things only: the even seventy
degrees at which Pullman interiors were maintained regard-
less of the plunging temperatures without, and the nearly
six feet square of living space afforded by the design and
placement of the deep plush seats. A tall man for his time,
Fulwider luxuriated in the ability to stretch his long, thin
limbs without disturbing the passenger seated next to him.

The pair had been companions since Fargo, and yet

scarcely a word had passed between them since their meeting, when the easterner had determined that the rangy old fellow with the ill-fitting suit and massive handlebars was returning to his ranch in Idaho from a cattle-buying trip to Grand Forks. He, in turn, had learned nothing about the man from New York beyond the fact that he was out here on business. If the cattleman was curious about this pale and rather emaciated traveler who appeared to be in his early forties, and who drew out a silk handkerchief from time to time to cough decorously into its folds, he gave no indication.

At length Fulwider grew bored with the sameness of the flat scenery and returned his attention to his fellow passenger.

"I thought you cowboys generally did your buying down in Texas." Traces of his New Hampshire beginnings lingered in his pronunciation of *thought* and *down*, which came out *thot* and *don*.

"I'm a foreman, not a cowboy." The westerner studied his watch, snapped shut the face and returned it to his vest pocket. His great grizzled moustaches appeared by their sheer weight to be dragging his sun-browned flesh away from the bone. "The man we're buying from owns the only complete herd of Herefords in the country. Ranch manager wants to breed out the Texas longhorn strain." His tone was derogatory.

"It doesn't sound as if you agree," said his companion.

"I reckon what I think don't much matter."

For a while they rode in silence. Steel wheels clicked rhythmically over the joints in the rails. "Have you ever been in Deadwood?" Fulwider asked then.

"Been there."

"I'm going to write about it. R. G. Fulwider. I work for the *World*." He proffered his hand.

The foreman grasped it. His palm was dry and horny with calluses. "Dale Crippen. What's the R. G. stand for?"

"My parents never told me. I've been assigned to do a series about the West. Mr. Pulitzer feels we've been ignoring what he calls 'an untapped vein of pure gold for the journalist.' Confidentially, he's jealous because the *Herald* scooped him on a serial based on the life of Jesse James and picked up five thousand new readers. So I'm on my way to write about Wild Bill Hickok. I'm supposed to get off at Bismarck and take the stage south to Deadwood. That's where he was killed, you know."

"Ten years ago," Crippen pointed out.

"It didn't seem to make any difference to readers of the *Herald* that Jesse James has been in the ground four years," said the journalist. "What's it like in the Black Hills?"

"It ain't like New York."

Fulwider waited for more, but none was forthcoming. Deciding his companion wasn't in the mood for conversation, he sank back in his seat and resumed his morose scrutiny of the tabletop country beyond the thick window.

"This here is what you ought to write about," said Crippen.

Turning back, the easterner was handed an eight-by-eleven sheet of stiff white posterboard. He had wondered about the bundle wrapped in brown paper on the seat between them, but had been too polite to ask what it was. The top line was printed in bold black capitals.

### $600 REWARD $600

For the Whole Hide, or other Proof of Death or Capture, of a Black-Mantled Wolf weighing in excess of 100 pounds, and known as Black Jack, Leader of a

Large Pack in the Caribou Foothills whose Depredations among local Herds of Cattle and Wild Game have been the Source of much Concern among the Good Citizens of Rebellion.

## $5 BOUNTY $5

For each Wolf Scalp taken in the Vicinity of the Snake River Valley, or more than Twice what the Territory of Idaho is offering for the same Item. Redeemable from any Member of the Idaho Stockmen's Association.

Nelson Meredith,
President

Meredith's signature was a daring indigo slash above the printed name.

"I mean to tack some of these up at every stop 'twixt here and Rebellion," the foreman announced, as the leaflet was returned.

"Who is Nelson Meredith, besides the president of the Idaho Stockmen's Association?" asked Fulwider.

"Englishman who runs the Newcastle spread. He pays my salary."

"He must be a crown prince, or at least an earl. Six hundred dollars seems rather a stiff bounty to pay for a wolf."

"Not for this wolf."

The conversation swung back to Deadwood, which Crippen said was an ugly collection of ramshackle huts and tents that leaked during the rainy season and stank to high heaven when the weather was warm, and where a man had to shake scorpions out of his boots each morning before pulling them on.

"What you want to go there for anyway?" he concluded. "No one's there who knew Wild Bill. They all drifted on when the claims started drying up."

"Well, I don't really have to write about Hickok. That was just one of the suggestions. I'm mainly here to find colorful characters whose life stories would interest our readers." He didn't mention the real reason why he had sought the wide open spaces. Thus far, no one west of Park Row knew that Fulwider was a consumptive, and that was the way he would have it.

"You won't find nothing down there but digger injuns and panhandlers." The foreman used a folding knife to saw an inch and a half off a tobacco plug he had taken from a coat pocket and popped it into his mouth. Immediately a black porter in a white coat appeared with a cuspidor of gleaming brass, set it at the passenger's feet and was gone. "What you ought to do is come out to Rebellion with me. Bet you find someone there worth making famous."

"What sort of place is Rebellion?"

"Well, it ain't New York neither, but nothing's made from canvas and you won't have to shake varmints out of your boots."

"If there's a hotel and a place to get a drink I'll consider it," Fulwider said.

A mischievous glint lit up the cattleman's faded blue eyes, set deep in a forest of cracks. "Man after my own heart," he chuckled, and poked a bony elbow into the journalist's ribs that sent him into a violent coughing fit. Concerned, Crippen drew back the offending arm. "That's a bad cold."

"It's an allergy." The reply was muffled by the wadded handkerchief.

"Maybe Idaho ain't the place for you, then. In springtime the Snake River Valley's nothing but grass and flowers."

Fulwider glanced at the handkerchief, wiped his eyes and put it away. "I'm told altitudes are just what this kind of allergy requires."

"Well, then, Rebellion's your place. The valley's three thousand feet above sea level. Last time we buried a farmer it was because he fell off his potato patch."

In Bismarck the train stopped to take on wood and water, and the two travelers repaired to a respectable-looking saloon on a street of rutted mud frozen hard as granite. A stiff breeze gnawed at their faces as, hands deep in their overcoat pockets, they dodged heavy horse and wagon traffic, bounded across the boardwalk and plunged through the doorway onto a sawdust floor.

It was early afternoon, and the establishment was all but empty. Fulwider warmed himself at a rusty stove in the corner while Crippen ordered a bottle and two glasses from a bearded, bear-like bartender and brought them to a nearby table. For twenty minutes they sat drinking, the Newcastle foreman trying to explain how they would transfer from the Northern Pacific to the Oregon Short Line, by which means they would proceed to Rebellion. The journalist paid scant attention. He had already made up his mind to accompany the older man.

Had he been interested enough to notice, the casual customer might have wondered at the relationship between the unlikely pair. Apart from their dependency on alcohol they had little in common. One had lived all but the first six of his fifty years west of the Rockies (for so Crippen narrated between descriptions of what lay ahead of them as the whiskey loosened his tongue), fought Indians and Mexicans, been shot twice and driven more beef to market than the average man could envision. The other, ten years his junior,

had grown up on the Atlantic Coast and spent most of his
adult life with fellow journalists and ward politicians. No
foundation existed upon which they could build a healthy
discussion, and yet from the beginning each felt an un-
shakeable bond developing.

Fulwider was refilling their glasses when the door
opened to admit a gust of arctic air and a figure that awakened his reporter's instincts as suddenly as a whiff of smoke
or a cry of murder.

It was not the stranger's savage costume that caught his
eye, though the tattered wolfskin hanging below his knees
and floppy-brimmed fur hat with a black-tipped eagle's
feather in the band would have been singular enough back
home. Rather, it was the way the man moved.

Broken down to its basic elements, his stride as he approached the bar was not properly a stride at all, but rather
a fluid display of well-toned muscles working in perfect
coordination, as smooth and graceful as water sliding over
rock. The journalist was tempted to describe it as sailor's
roll, except that there was not enough sway in the shoulders
and there was nothing remotely nautical about the man. It
was animal-like, the slouching gait of a dog or a big cat.
Or a wolf.

"Do you know that fellow?" asked Fulwider, taking advantage of a lull in his companion's monologue.

Scowling at this irrelevance, the foreman craned his head
around to peer in the direction indicated. He was still
scowling when he turned back.

"Some wolfer," he said sourly, and drank. "I can smell
him clear over here."

The journalist thought this an exaggeration, but when he
redirected his attention to the newcomer he became aware
of a faint, foul stench reminiscent of dead rats in an alley.
It wasn't lost upon one of the two men beside whom the

man was standing at the bar, who sniffed loudly and set down his glass with a "Pah!"

The stranger, whose medium height barely brought his hat brim to the bridge of the thick-built brute's nose, ignored him and ordered whiskey in a quiet voice barely audible across the room.

"Jim," called the brute, louder than necessary to be heard by the imbiber at his other elbow, "there's a real bad stink in here. You reckon something crawled into the beer keg and died?"

"It do smell like that's the case." His partner gulped at his foaming glass and drew a faded gingham sleeve across his mouth. Constructed along slimmer lines than his companion, he was every bit as tall. "I thought it was you."

"No, Sir. Way I see it, a man that don't bathe before he goes out in public, he's worse'n a hydrophoby skunk. That the way you see it, Jim?"

"That's the way I see it, Aaron."

"How about you, Mister?" Aaron sneered at the stranger.

He went on drinking and gazing at nothing in particular behind the bar. The bartender had moved to the far end, and a fourth customer who had been standing beside the one called Jim had paid for his beer and left. Suddenly Aaron inhaled again and reeled back as if struck, holding his broken lump of a nose between thumb and forefinger.

"Holy Christ!" he exclaimed, feigning shock. "I just found our hydrophoby skunk!"

The target of his jibes flicked a finger at his empty shot glass. The bartender moved in reluctantly to refill it, spilling some of the red-tinted liquid, then retreated to his position of safety.

"Mister," the brute bored in, "do you know what folks in these parts do to mad skunks?"

"I wouldn't," warned the other calmly.

"Wouldn't what, Mister?" Aaron backed away. His hand fell to the butt of a revolver nosing above his belt. His stomach hung out on either side of it like dough escaping a pan.

"Wouldn't what, Mister?" He tugged at the curved handle.

Afterward, Fulwider was unable to say for certain what happened next, even though like everyone else in the room he was watching closely. One second the man in the wolfskin was leaning on his elbows with his back turned, and the next he and Aaron were facing each other across two feet and something was shining in the stranger's hand and the brute was clutching his abdomen and watching incredulously as something bright red oozed between his fingers. The gun was still in his belt.

His partner stared from one face to the other, still uncomprehending. Then his eyes fell to Aaron's stomach and color fled his face.

"Get him to a doctor," the man in pelts told him. He might have been ordering a third whiskey for all the emotion his tone betrayed.

Jim was unarmed. His gaze was riveted on the skinning knife's double-edged blade, where his friend's blood was trickling down the sloped edges in twin rivulets. Then he threw a supporting arm around Aaron's hunched shoulders and helped him toward the door—the latter, his mouth forming a silent *o*, allowing himself to be led out like a tame fawn.

"Bar towel." The knife-wielder held out his free hand to the bartender. When the drink-sopped rag was in his possession he wiped the blade clean, then discarded the towel and dried the weapon on his wolfskin before returning it to its sheath behind his back. Fulwider noticed then that the fur was split for easy access to the hilt.

"Don't move."

The stranger had been turning back to the bar when the lean man entered, wearing a corduroy coat with a shaggy collar and a fur hat. He carried a short-barreled shotgun and had a star pinned to his lapel. His quarry froze while he drew near and reached out to disarm the man in pelts.

"Who are you?" demanded the lawman, holding the knife down at his side. He wore a thick black moustache with tips waxed shiny.

"North."

"North? Is that your name or the direction you came from?" There was no reply. "Since when is having a little fun with a stranger a capital offense?"

"Since when is pulling a gun on a man having a little fun?" North watched his reflection in a clouded mirror behind the bar. It was an ordinary face, sunburned and a little stubbled.

"Anybody see that?" The lawman's eyes flicked around the room, sharp as pinpoints.

Only two customers remained besides Fulwider and Crippen. No one spoke. The bartender was busily polishing a glass with a fresh towel.

"Let's go." The shotgun nuzzled North's back.

"Oh, Christ." Crippen flashed the journalist a sour look and pushed himself out of his seat.

The lawman watched warily as he approached and stopped six feet short of prisoner and captor.

"He's telling it true, Marshal. The big one went for a Peacemaker. North could of kilt him, but he didn't. If you got to arrest him for something, arrest him for that."

"You saw that?" The other's face was a blank slab.

"Seen the whole thing. Him too." The foreman indicated Fulwider, who raised his empty glass in uneasy acknowledgment.

The marshal took a deep breath and clapped the wolfer's knife down on the bar beyond his reach. "You figure on staying long?" he snarled.

"No longer than I got to." North resumed drinking. He had not looked at the lawman once.

"Make it short." He left, banging the door behind him.

Crippen returned to the table without so much as a word to the wolfer. A train whistle blew hoarsely, setting glasses and bottles buzzing. "That's us," he told Fulwider.

The journalist accompanied him to the door. "He might at least have thanked you."

"That'd be like thanking a man for not stealing your poke."

On his way out, the man from New York made a mental note to work the rejoinder into a future article for the *World*.

# TWO

There were no Pullmans on the Oregon Short Line. After three days of racketing over the rails in a swaying coach, Fulwider was grateful when the train whooshed to a halt amid a cluster of dark log buildings that looked as if they had started out weary and had long since sunk past despair into tragic resignation. A moldy sky hung so low over the rooftops it seemed a man might reach up and grab a handful if he thought he could wash it off right away.

"Will we be stopped long enough to stretch our legs?" he asked Crippen, who was unfolding his lanky frame from his hard hickory seat.

"Long enough to stretch them or shrink them or do anything you like with them," replied his companion, dragging down a dilapidated leather satchel from the overhead rack. "This here's Rebellion."

Fulwider's heart sank. Huddled between the Caribou and Big Hole mountains on the twisting thread of water that gave the Snake River Valley its name, the dowdy structures were scattered willy-nilly across a mud hollow, with no sign of a street or even a placard to identify them as anything but another of the depressing bone-pickers' shanty-towns he had observed previously along the right-of-way.

A terrible dread seized him as he carried his bags onto the platform—not of death or danger, which would merely have stimulated the creative impulse that had brought him, but that his health would not return as quickly as he hoped and that he should have to spend the rest of his days amid such cruel boredom.

"Is it always like this?" he asked Crippen. A handful of bearded men in patched logging jackets stood on the platform, but made no move to greet the only two passengers who had alighted. The journalist suspected that watching the train come in was the highlight of their day.

"Why, hell, no," said the cowhand, around today's tobacco plug. "It will be like this here for a couple of days at the most, and then things will settle down and get downright dismal for a while."

The hotel was a square, three-story frame building, one of only two in the log village, whose sign running the length of the front porch identified it as the Assiniboin Inn. Though it was of fairly recent construction, the paint on one of the porch pillars came off in a grayish dust on Fulwider's sleeve when he brushed against it, and orange rust coated the iron sconces in which a lantern rested on either side of the door. Before going in, Crippen got his hammer and sack of nails from his satchel and fixed a fresh poster to the front of the building, which from the many other bills that already decorated it appeared to be something of a community bulletin board.

During the operation, Fulwider asked about the stench that seemed to be coming from a crooked alley winding behind the Assiniboin. Overpowering, it reminded him of the man in Bismarck.

"Pelts," came the reply. "That's where they tally them before paying out bounties. This here is the wolfing capital of the Northwest."

Far from elegant, the hotel lobby nonetheless carried a simple dignity in its sturdy design and utilitarian furnishings to which no amount of gilt fixtures or burgundy carpeting could add. A broad staircase of hand-rubbed oak led to the upper floors on the other side of a large desk. Behind this beamed a middle-aged clerk with a round, florid face and blond hair brushed back from a scanty widow's peak. When Crippen greeted him, Fulwider learned that the man's Christian name, unfortunately, was Thanatopsis.

"Is he in?" asked the foreman, after fielding a number of questions about his trip.

The clerk nodded. "With the others. He said to send you right up."

Crippen started in that direction, leaving behind the satchel. "Keep an eye on that. And take good care of my friend here from back East."

The journalist registered, assuring the clerk that R. G. stood for nothing, and carried his own bags upstairs after ascertaining that there was no bell captain. A number of men passed him on their way down.

Older men all, they wore suits of varying quality under knee-length overcoats and headgear ranging from derbies like Fulwider's to the storied ten-gallon Stetson, which had proven rarer out West than he had been led to believe. There was not a clean-shaven lip among them. To a man they moved with that air of being late for an important appointment that the journalist had so often noted in financiers on their way and from the stock exchange.

Dale Crippen was on Fulwider's floor, deep in conversation with a square-rigged man who stood in an open doorway with his back to a room full of chairs upholstered in dark leather. As the easterner drew near, Crippen stopped in midsentence to introduce them.

Nelson Meredith was solid-looking, with a square face

admirably suited for his sidewhiskers, and a head of thick,
wavy auburn hair going silver at the temples. His suit was
cut western style, his high boots tilted forward on two-inch
heels and hand-tooled Mexican fashion, but Fulwider suspected that nothing like them was available in town, or
anywhere else west of New Bond Street. He had a firm
handshake and ruthless blue eyes that took in the new ac-
quaintance from sole to crown.

"I hope you will enjoy your stay in my Idaho." His
cultured English accent softened the rather jarring effect of
the possessive pronoun.

The journalist responded with an inanity, and explained
the official reason for his visit. Meredith laughed softly, a
low, silken rumble that barely stirred the lines of his face.

"I fear that you will be disappointed," he said. "The
sort of creature you are hunting no longer exists out here,
if indeed he ever did. There is but one Wild Bill Hickok
to a century."

"And yet I've reason to believe that others of his ilk are
still available, if one is willing to look for them." Briefly
he recounted the incident in the Bismarck saloon.

"North?" repeated the rancher, raising his eyebrows.
"*Asa* North? The wolfer?"

"Sweet Jesus!" Crippen placed a hand to his high, bald
forehead. "I never thought to put them together!"

Noting Fulwider's bewilderment, Meredith explained:
"You'd have no way of knowing back East, but out here
Asa North is a legend. Among his many exploits, he is said
to have killed more than a hundred wolves with his bare
hands. As the story goes, he chases the creature on
horseback until it has no place to run, then calmly dis-
mounts, seizes it by the muzzle and snaps its neck with a
jerk."

"Sort of a frontier Paul Bunyan," laughed the other appreciatively.

"Exactly! Except that you are the first men I've met who claim to have seen him in person."

"Just as soon not have," grumbled Crippen.

Amusement glittered in the rancher's otherwise cold blue eye. "Dale considers wolfers a necessary evil at best."

"Filthy lot, as a rule," said the other and hesitated with a glance in the journalist's direction. "This ain't going to show up in print, is it? I heard of folks being throwed in jail for talking about other folks."

"I'll consider anything you say as strictly off the record," Fulwider assured him.

"If that means you ain't going to write down what I say, all right." He shifted his plug from one cheek to the other, an action his traveling partner of the past few days had learned to recognize as a signal of garrulity. "I never knowed a puncher who didn't earn some spare money wolfing. Done it myself, plenty of times. But professional wolfers are something different, and North is the worst of them. No one can touch him in kills, but the rest of us manage to snag our share of the bastards without becoming one of them."

"Nevertheless, there's a vein of truth in the most implausible myths," argued the journalist. "If what he did to that bully in the saloon is an indication of his performance under stress, I'd say he's just the man to hunt down your Black Jack."

This bit of reasoning was met with an icy silence. Meredith turned a face to his foreman from which all the good humor had drained.

"That's one of the things we discussed at the meeting just now," he said. "Black Jack's in business again. He struck the Harper ranch two nights running, and last night he got Old Abe on Newcastle property.''

Crippen let fly with a remarkable string of curses. He had spoken of the steer called Old Abe aboard the train, an enormous longhorn used as lead animal by the present ranch manager's father, Sir William Meredith, on his first cattle drive from Texas fifteen years before. Though the beasts were generally held in contempt by men forced to spend much time with them, Fulwider had noted a grudging respect in the foreman's description of Abe's unerring sense of direction and unchallenged mastery of the herd.

''Sure it was Jack?'' Crippen asked, when he had finally run out of oaths. His face was bright red.

''The line rider got a shot at a white wolf lingering near the carcass. The only one like that around here is his mate, and they're always together.'' The Englishman paused. ''The others are in favor of doubling the bounty.''

His employee shook his head fiercely. ''Don't much like that idea. Twelve hunnert dollars'd bring in too much scum.''

''That's what I told the others. They agreed to wait and see what the six hundred dollar offer brings.''

Nothing more was said on the subject, and when Meredith turned back to the journalist he was once again the genial cattle baron. ''Well, I certainly hope you find your hero.'' He extended his hand.

Clearly this was a dismissal. In parting, Fulwider said, ''Heroes need not be gunmen. I'm certain our readers would be just as eager to learn about big ranchers such as yourself.''

''I would disappoint them. My father came to this territory when it was populated only by red Indians and herds of buffalo who were unimpressed by his knighthood. He carved out an empire larger than some European kingdoms

with his bare hands and a little help from Mr. Colt. I, however, was educated at Cambridge and moved here only ten
years ago upon his death.'' He smiled complacently. ''I am
something of a carpetbagger, you see.''

Fulwider's lungs were beginning to close up. He made
a hasty end to the interview and took leave. He barely got
to his room with his luggage when the terrible racking began.

When it was done he sat down weakly on the edge of
the bed and inspected his handkerchief. As yet there was
no blood. Unstrapping his portmanteau, he excavated a
quart bottle of gin from among his shirts, uncorked it and
tipped it up to dissolve the phlegm in his throat. It worked
admirably. His problem was that he didn't stop once it had
accomplished its purpose.

The sun was past its peak when he awoke next day, spread-
eagled on top of the covers and fully dressed. There was a
dull throbbing behind his eyes that increased when he
opened them, and the smell coming from behind the hotel
seemed to have settled in his mouth in the form of a vile
taste. The empty bottle thudded to the floor when he got
up.

His bladder was swelled to bursting. Emptying it into a
white enamel chamber pot discovered under the bed, he
remembered seeing a saloon across from the hotel on his
way in. With the aid of the dresser mirror he made himself
as presentable as possible without shaving—his hands
weren't to be trusted yet—lowered his hat carefully onto
his fragile head and struck out for the hallway.

Rutted paths charitably referred to as streets described
twisting passages among the buildings. He started across a
plank thoughtfully provided for the more fastidious pedes-
trians, only to hold back when a lone horseman attired in

a bulky coat came along at a weary walk, hoofs squishing in the six-inch-deep mud. When horse and rider had passed he resumed walking, then stopped again.

He blinked at the man's retreating back. His headache was blinding and the sun breaking through the cloud cover overhead was too bright for his gin-blurred eyes to make out anything beyond vague shadows. But there was no mistaking that stench.

# THREE

Fortified by two glasses of inferior whiskey and a shave at the barber shop, operated by a German who knew almost no words of English and doubled as the owner of the livery stable, the journalist felt closer to human as he re-entered the Assiniboin. He could think of only one reason why Asa North was in Rebellion—Meredith's bounty offer for Black Jack's skin.

The clerk looked fresh in a recently turned collar and beaver coat beginning to show wear at the elbows. His servile smile when greeting Fulwider was a welcome change from the condescending leer he had grown to expect from eastern concierges after observing his condition on the way out.

"Is Nelson Meredith still registered?" he asked.

"He checked out this morning, sir. Gone back to Newcastle. He only stays in town once or twice a month when the ranchers meet. Mr. Crippen left for the ranch last night."

"Has anyone else asked for him within the past hour?"

A disturbed expression flashed across the hotel employee's features. "Yes, a rather vile person in a fur vest.

He was quite fragrant. I told him the same thing I told you.''

''What did he say?''

''He said it didn't make any difference. Do you know him?''

''No, but I'd like to. Did he mention where he was going?''

''He's registered.'' Thanatopsis spun the thick book lying open on the counter so that the guest could read the signatures. The name he was looking for was written in a clerkly hand next to a bold X and the date. ''Room Fourteen. I thought it best to put at least a floor between him and the other guests.''

The door stood open, allowing sunlight onto the rubber runner that answered for a carpet in the hallway. Wondering if the wolfer was asleep after his long ride, Fulwider crept on tiptoe along the wall and stepped inside, fist poised to rap on the jamb.

The window had been flung up and the room was full of early spring chill. The furniture was identical to that in his own quarters, including a brass bed with a thick, flower-print counterpane, unoccupied at present. The room was deserted. He was about to leave when something cold and rigid touched the bone behind his right ear. The dry air was split by a metallic snap.

''That there was the set trigger,'' whispered a voice at the same ear. ''All's I got to do to make the other one go off is think about it. Maybe you'll want to take my mind off it by talking. Don't turn around!''

The warning lashed out like a serpent's tongue. As the journalist had started to turn, he glimpsed North, naked to the waist, standing behind the door. He froze at the command.

''What should I talk about?'' The effects of his morning

session with the bottle were gone, as if drained down the barrel of the rifle.

"You can start with why you was sneaking up on a man in his room."

"I was trying to be quiet. I thought you were sleeping."

"I was. Now I'm not."

"Your door was open."

"Don't like being closed in."

Fulwider introduced himself. He had raised his hands without realizing that he was doing so. "I'm a journalist. A newspaper writer. I have cards inside my coat."

"Take your word for it."

"I'd like very much to have a few words with you, Mr. North. I'm not armed." He suppressed a gasp as a crusty hand came up beneath his coat and groped about with a practiced, expert touch. When it was withdrawn:

"Where'd you hear my name?"

"In a saloon in Bismarck," he blurted, in his anxiety answering the question literally. "Last week. I'm certain you saw me."

"I see a lot of folks, more than I care to. What makes you special?"

"The fellow I was with helped you out of a close spot with the marshal. A tall old cowhand with a gray moustache."

"Turn around."

The journalist obeyed, and the rifle was lowered. Face to face he was surprised to see that he was two inches taller than the wolfer. Even allowing for the minimal advantage given him by his low heels over a man in his stocking feet, the difference was startling and a trifle disconcerting. He had expected more of a legend.

The man was not physically striking. His face was seamed and browned beyond what Fulwider judged to be its thirty years, so that the flesh clung to the bone the way a square of ancient carpet long past design embraces a floor, taking on the shape, color and texture of the boards beneath, but this quality was shared by hundreds of farmers and cattlemen between the Ohio River and the Barbary Coast. Hatless, he had a broad forehead divided by a low widow's peak the color of wet buckskin, darker than the rest of his hair, which was gathered into a sandy queue behind his neck. His eyes were a curious amber, the shade of properly aged brandy, but in spite of a disturbing note in their bland scrutiny they were easily wasted upon the unobservant. A v of coarse hair to match the widow's peak matted his broad torso between flat breasts.

Fulwider tried not to notice the animal smell he exuded even with his death-tainted garments hanging on the bedpost a yard away, but in all honesty this was his most notable attribute.

North filled his lungs in a slow draft and emptied them in a short whoosh through his nostrils. His gun, a rifle with a thirty-inch octagonal barrel and ornate scrollwork on the receiver, revolved slowly until its muzzle was almost touching the floor. The hammer was replaced with a metallic crunch. A firearms enthusiast, Fulwider identified it from its blue-green cast as a 38-55 Ballard No. 4, a formidable weapon.

"You'd stomped up them stairs like anyone else I wouldn't of even woke up," said the wolfer. "Folks that walk quiet bother me." He fell silent. After a moment the journalist realized that he was expected to speak.

"As I said, I'm a journalist," he began haltingly. "I'm on assignment from the New York *World* to interview and write about our modern frontiersmen. From what I have heard about you, I would say you're the first one I've met who is worth the ink and paper."

"What'd you hear?"

He repeated the wolf-strangling story Meredith had told him. North grunted.

"That one's been following me for years. Wolves don't wrestle. They run when you get near them. If there's room."

"And if there isn't?"

"I kill them. With this." He raised and lowered the Ballard.

"I see." The answer disappointed Fulwider. He went on to tell him what he had acquired from Dale Crippen on the subject of North.

"That what folks like to read about these days?" he asked. "Don't sound like it'd hardly fill up a page."

"That is why I wish to interview you."

"Don't expect me to read it. I don't read nor write. Never seen the percentage."

"That won't be necessary." The journalist felt his confidence returning. If he had learned one fact in his career it was that everyone wanted to be famous. "When can we start?"

"Start what?" North leaned the rifle against the wall beside the bed.

"Why, the interview. I'll have to ask you some questions."

"How long does that take?"

Fulwider frowned. "An hour. Perhaps longer. It depends on what you have to tell me."

"Sorry." The wolfer sat down on the edge of the bed and started pulling on a tired-looking pair of calf-length moccasins decorated with porcupine quills dyed red and yellow.

"What do you mean?"

"Can't spare it. I got to get provisions and a fresh pack

animal. One I had got stole in Bismarck. Then I got to ride out to Newcastle and see can I parley this Meredith into upping the bounty on this here wolf he wants so bad. One way or the other I'm going hunting in the morning.''

"Then we can talk when you get back."

"If you care to wait." He drew his stiff buckskin shirt on over his head.

"How long?"

"Day, maybe. More likely a month. Time don't mean much to me, except when it's short."

"Can't you be more specific?" Fulwider struggled to keep his frustration from showing. Westerners had no concept of deadlines or the impatience of editors.

Standing, North drew on the heavy wolfskin and lifted his beaver hat from the bedpost. From scalp to sole nothing touched his skin that was made by man. "That's up to Black Jack."

The journalist felt an attack coming on, but got out his handkerchief in time to stifle it. The effort brought tears to his eyes, but he had a proposition to make and didn't want to discredit it by exhibiting the state of his health.

"Take me with you."

For a space the wolfer favored him with his disconcerting gaze. Then he put on the hat. "I reckon not."

"Don't turn me down until you've heard me out. I can ride and am perfectly capable of taking care of myself. I have been, for more years than you have been alive."

"Years don't mean nothing. You stink city, Mr. Fulwider. There ain't no corner markets in the mountains."

He couldn't hold back his anger any longer. "You can stop me from accompanying you, but nothing says I can't follow you."

The wolfskin rustled. In a trice, North's wicked skinning

knife was out and pricking Fulwider's flesh above his belt buckle.

"That's the first wrong thing you said since you come in, Mr. Newspaper Writer." He spoke in that deceptively calm tone he had used after letting out the bully's intestines in the Dakota barroom. "It's up to you whether you leave here straight up or heels first. If I look back and see you on my trail I'll flay you breathing."

Fulwider left, backing away on unsteady legs.

For a long time after returning to his room, the journalist sat on the edge of his bed while his hands shook and his heart hammered at his breastbone. Then he unpacked his bags, transferring his clothes to the dresser slowly and methodically. When he was certain the wolfer had completed his business in town and started out for Newcastle he went out to get the lay of the community.

After an hour he had visited every public building but one. A twin of the Assiniboin, this frame structure was known locally as Aurora's place although it bore no sign. Frilly curtains in its windows concealed the sort of activity one might expect of an establishment referred to as "the other side of Sin." He avoided such places out of revulsion sparked by weeks of personal debauchery following his bitter divorce two years before. He considered it a healthy sign, however, that the townsmen with whom he conversed spoke freely and knowledgeably about the services available there. Evidently, eastern hypocrisy had yet to move beyond the 98th Meridian.

Most of all, Fulwider was struck by the dearth of women in town. In New York they outnumbered the men, but here (not counting Aurora's girls) there were at least fifteen males to every female. He had heard of soldiers stationed in frontier outposts drawing lots to see which troopers would allow themselves to be led at dances, but until now he had never understood their desperation. An avowed misogynist since the end of his own marriage, the newcomer was nonetheless depressed by the loss of his freedom of choice.

The sun was perched atop the buttes west of town when he entered the local restaurant, a cramped place in the same building with the Timber Queen saloon, separated from it by a pine partition and run by a former trail cook with a peg leg and an apparently unsinkable sense of humor. Fulwider was just starting in on a surprisingly delectable beef stew when he spotted Dale Crippen in the doorway. He hailed the foreman with fork upraised.

"Find any Wyatt Earps yet?" asked Crippen, seating himself opposite the journalist.

"I may have found someone much better, if I could get him to cooperate." He told of the conversation in North's room, pausing only when the cook stumped over to take his companion's order.

"He showed up at the ranch this afternoon," said Crippen, when Fulwider had finished. His scowl was ferocious. "Talked Nelson into doubling the bounty on Black Jack. Old Man Meredith wouldn't of went for it, but his son is too full of dime-novel nonsense and thinks North is Pecos Bill all over again."

"I'm not quite clear yet on what you have against North."

The speedy arrival of the foreman's dinner lightened his mood somewhat, and between jokes about its being the first veal he'd ever eaten that had died of old age, he described the wolfing process.

Most wolfers, Fulwider was informed, were cowboys let go during the long winter months. Equipped with guns, pack horses and a minimum of supplies, these stalwarts would venture into the wilderness at the first sign of snow and not be seen again until the thaw, when they returned laden with gray furs and redeemed them for the bounty. As likely as not, they would immediately throw away this boon at the local saloon or hospitable house and be back at the ranch next morning to prepare for spring round-up.

The rest were professionals, who appeared at the onset of winter festooned with leg-traps and strangling-snares, then vanished after the season's bounty was collected. They were an ornery, odious class shunned for their ill manners and distrust of soap. Crippen considered Asa North among this category.

"Tell me something about wolves," said the easterner, fascinated by this glimpse into a world he hadn't known existed.

"I reckon if the Devil ever decides to visit, he'll come dressed as a wolf." The foreman used a biscuit to mop the last of the gravy from his plate. "A live one on the loose is worth a couple of thousand dollars in lost livestock every winter. The rule out here is that no self-respecting cattleman will pass by a carcass without stopping to poison it and maybe account for at least one lofer."

"Lofer?"

"One of the kindlier names for the bastards. Who knows where these things start? Anyway, the trade in pelts hereabouts is lively. They make fine coats. Ever seen one of these?" He drew a pouch from his hip pocket and extended it.

The journalist fondled the leather-like sack. Black, it was drawn with a thong and despite the thinness of the material it seemed sturdy though well worn.

"Wolf scrotum. You won't find hardly a cowboy or a cattleman who don't keep his smoking tobacco in one like it. I don't use the stuff, but it makes just as good a poke. Been carrying this one ten years. Can't wear it out."

Fulwider quickly returned the item. "What about Black Jack?"

"You got to admire him," Crippen replied grudgingly. "He's the leader of a pack that comes down from the Caribous now and again and plays hell with every herd in the valley. It's been three years now, some say five, and no one's nailed him yet. He ain't your ordinary lofer. He thinks."

"Is he any match for someone like North?"

He pushed away his empty plate. "Reckon I'll know that soon enough. I'm going along."

"How'd you get him to agree to that?" asked the other, astonished.

"That was Meredith's only condition for kicking up the bounty. He ain't forgot that I had to boot out a couple of wolfers I caught butchering Newcastle beef last year. Besides, I'm the only one ever put a bullet in Black Jack's hide."

"I thought you said no one ever had."

"Didn't say no such a thing. Shooting him and killing him ain't the same."

Fulwider acted on a hunch. "You'll need someone to take care of the pack animals. How about me?"

"You?" A smile, half amused and half exasperated, stirred the foreman's moustaches. "You wouldn't survive two days."

"Don't try to scare me. I've visited neighborhoods in New York where the murder rate is higher than in your Tombstone and Dodge City combined. Besides, you owe it to me to take me along."

"I owe you?" Crippen's face flushed deep copper.

"I came here on your suggestion," the journalist reminded him. "You said my chances of finding someone worth writing about here would be greater than in Deadwood. Now that I've found him you won't let me have a chance at him. Is all this I've heard about a westerner's word being his bond just another myth?''

Crippen rose, and for a moment Fulwider wondered if he was going to strike him. Then he got out his poke and placed money on the table for his meal. ''I'm meeting him in front of the hotel tomorrow, first light,'' he said. ''Be there if you want, but don't blame me when he kills you.'' He went out, leaving the other to ponder the remnants of his stew.

# FOUR

That evening, after many inquiries, Fulwider found someone who had the knowledge and was willing to give him advice about planning a wolfing trip, in return for a modest fee. This was a hideous old man with no teeth in a reeking little room above the livery stable who earned his keep shoveling out the stalls, and who used to wolf for Sir William Meredith before a fall from his horse crippled him. Afterward, the journalist used *World* expense money to purchase two horses downstairs and acquire sundry other necessaries just before the shops closed. He turned in early and was up well before dawn.

The sky was turning pale when he returned to the hotel leading the animals—one for riding, the other loaded down with packs—and carrying a 50-70 Remington rifle. He had exchanged his city finery for stiff denim trousers, boots, canvas jacket with fur collar and wide-brimmed felt hat, and was feeling very rugged. Among the smaller articles stored in his saddle pouches was a bottle of strychnine crystals, which he had been assured was the most essential item in a wolfer's gear.

North was tightening the strap that secured his own bare supplies to a muscular black with three white stockings.

The roan beside it was equally substantial, though a bit too short and thick in the haunches to please the fancier of fine horseflesh. Neither was as handsome as Fulwider's matched grays. Amber eyes glared at him over the packs.

"What the hell are you doing here?"

The New Yorker had spent much of the previous night in bed fashioning the very explanation that fled from him the instant he met North's gaze. Desperately he fished for words.

"I invited him."

The wolfer looked at Dale Crippen, mounted upon a sorrel mare and leading a great gaunt gray conspicuous like North's black for its lack of unwieldy bundles. He was packing a Colt revolver on his hip and a Henry repeating rifle in a saddle scabbard. He drew rein in front of the hotel, challenging North with his eyes.

"Did you think to invite a brass band?" The latter sliced through a dangling rope end with a single upward thrust of his fearsome knife. "I'm partial to slide trombones."

"I'll see to him. You just tend to business."

"He'll see to himself. In a wolf pack, when one member gets too old or too weak to hunt, he falls back and feeds on what the others leave. If he don't like it, they eat him. It's a good rule." He glanced back at Fulwider. "The minute you start yelping about home and Ma's cooking I'll cut you up in little pieces and swallow you raw."

"There will be no murder done on this hunt," Crippen warned.

"Ain't no murderers in the mountains. Just survivors."

North had one foot in the stirrup when two men straddling slat-sided paints trailing a lathered pack horse slouched in from the east and dismounted heavily in front of the saloon. One, his impassive features all but hidden in shadow beneath the brim of a tall black hat, caught sight of the trio as he was hitching up and said something to his partner. He had dark, shoulder-length hair and dead black eyes like empty wells. The other, a slight fellow in a derby and ankle-length buffalo coat, glanced in their direction briefly, then turned back and stood watching them for what seemed a full minute, the rising sun blazing off his round corrective lenses. He seemed particularly interested in North. Then they both stepped up onto the boardwalk and into the dark barroom, which was just opening for business.

"You serve liquor to injuns here?" North finished mounting.

"If that law was enforced here the Timber Queen would be a dress shop," snorted the foreman. "You'll go a long way in Rebellion before you find someone who don't have redskin blood in his veins."

"That include you?"

"I was born in Philadelphia."

Fulwider stepped into leather. Months had passed since he had last sat a horse and he was acutely conscious of the added height. "Do you know those men?" he asked Crippen.

The foreman spat. It crackled in the icy morning air. "Half-breeds. That was Dick Lightfoot in the big hat. The other's Sam Fire Eye. They're the wolfers I run off Newcastle for rustling last November. If I catch them at it again I'll see they get a decent burial." He clucked his tongue and the sorrel started forward. North was already moving.

It was iron-cold along the road that led to the Meredith ranch and the Caribous beyond, the sun's rheumatic climb over the crisp outline of the mountains having done little to dispel the clammy grip of a winter not yet done. The horses' hoofs rang when they struck bare earth frozen four feet down. Clouds of steam hung about their heads. Fulwider asked if this wasn't a dangerous time to be in the mountains.

Crippen said it was, and described the tempestuous break-up now in progress, the ice cracking apart with tremendous reports and snow outcroppings weighing several tons toppling with the force of runaway freight trains to crush trees and abandoned trappers' shacks below. "We won't be going that high, though," he assured the journalist. "Wolves generally stick to the flatlands till warm weather."

"Unless they're being chased," North put in.

The foreman made no response, and the three continued in silence for three or four miles.

"How much you know about this particular lofer?" Crippen asked then.

North was studying patches of snow along both sides of the sunken path they were following. "He can't be poisoned," he said. "Won't go near the meat. Been shot at, never hit bad enough to kill. Digs up traps and springs them. He and his pack answer for several hundred head a year."

"You been talking to someone."

"I heard the same story a thousand times, about a thousand other wolves. They all got names. In Montana it's Old Three Toes, in Oregon Gus, in Dakota Pegleg—they're all older than dirt and smarter than some men. It's said. Ranchers always give then names, like they was pets. Makes them easier to deal with, I reckon."

It was the cold, Fulwider thought, that drew Crippen out of his customary reticence on this occasion. It was he who kept the conversation from flagging, as North sank into monosyllable, and eventually to ill-tempered grunts.

"Running shot," the foreman said. "Winged him, right hip. I was using a single-shot Springfield and wasn't packing no side arm. He went down rolling, but by the time I got reloaded he was up again and gone through the pines north of Gray's Lake. Would of had him even then, but my horse got tangled in brush and pulled up lame. It was right after that I got the Colt and the Henry repeater. Ain't had a chance at him since.''

''How did you know it was Black Jack?'' asked the journalist.

''By his size, for one, and by his black mantle. Covers his head and shoulders like a hood. There's others big as him, and there's lots with as much black in their coats, but he's the only one that's both. Also I seen his mate later, a good-size bitch and damn near pure white, though I didn't get a shot. There ain't two that color in a hunnert miles. If you see a pack moving along a ridge half a mile off and one of them is white you can bet it's Jack that's leading them.''

They were a mile off the trail that swung east to Newcastle headquarters when North peeled off to the west for a hundred yards, dismounted, spent some minutes inspecting a ribbon of frozen gray slush and announced perfunctorily that he had found wolf tracks.

''How can you be certain?'' Fulwider interposed, after he and Crippen had cantered over to investigate. The prints in question were swollen by melting, and vague. ''This close to civilization, wouldn't it more likely be a dog?''

''No, sir.'' The foreman pointed. ''See where he stuck his hind paw in the track made by the front? Same over here. A dog's would be a couple of inches inside.''

''Old one,'' commented the wolfer, more to himself than to the others.

Crippen nodded. ''Or sick. Hydrophobic, maybe, though they are too blurred to say for sure. That would explain its being so close to folks. They don't scare when they're like that."

Fulwider wondered if some bizarre frontier joke was being carried out at his expense. "You aren't saying that you can determine whether a wolf is old or sick just by its track!" he demanded.

No one replied. Crippen was watching North. "Which way you reckon?"

The wolfer's eyes searched the sky to the south, a leprous silver over the mountains. Finally he pointed at a jagged peak that resembled a dog's molar. "There. Heading west."

The foreman nodded again and leaned over in his saddle to spit. "Figures. They been doing most of their killing down by the lake."

Fulwider squinted in that direction, but could see nothing beyond a flock of birds flapping westward. From this distance it might have been a swarm of mosquitoes.

"How far to the river?" North asked.

Crippen studied him, chewing. The upper half of his face was obscured by the shadow of his Stetson, leaving only his moustache and working jowl visible. "Ten, twelve miles. How'd you know there was one?"

"Lakes don't just drop down like manure. They got to be fed." He mounted. "We'll camp just this side, cross over first light."

Days were short at that elevation. It was well past dark by the time they reached the river, where moonlight slid along the rippling surface at the base of a gentle grade. The journalist, who hadn't eaten since the night before, forgot his hunger as he dismounted and pain rushed to every muscle and joint in a body pampered by years of streetcar travel. He had never before known what it was like to be too exhausted to eat.

While the others were strapping nosebags over their horses' necks and building a fire, he hoisted out the quart bottle he had wrapped carefully and stored in a saddle pouch and drank deeply. Relief and contentment poured into the abused regions of his frame as he pushed the cork back in and returned the vessel to its hiding place.

He was undoing his cinch when a mournful cry arose from somewhere, literally raising the hairs on the back of his neck.

At first it sounded solitary, like a lone steam whistle hooting in a tunnel miles away, but as it climbed in pitch it splintered into a chorus of gulping ululations that seemed to issue from everywhere and yet nowhere. At length the other cries began to fall away until there was only one long, clear, billowing note that rose and sank and rose until it ceased to exist. When it did, the blend was so smooth that it was a moment before he could be sure he was no longer hearing it.

"Gathering the pack," said Crippen, after a long stillness. The sound of his voice made Fulwider start. The foreman resumed adding deadwood to the small pile he had ignited in the center of the clearing, but his subdued tone suggested that he had been affected no less than the journalist by the weird serenade. North's reactions were concealed in the shadows which enveloped the upper half of his body.

"Are you sure that fire will be large enough?" Fulwider asked then.

# FIVE

The cold lay like metal against the journalist's flesh when Crippen roused him with a surly toe into a pitch blackness relieved only by a patch of metallic gray over the eastern horizon. The horses stamped and blew thick clouds of milky vapor in the uneven light of a fire the size of a man's fist, over which North sat hunched watching something that sizzled in a cast iron skillet. The acrid smell of frying fat clashed with the odors of damp wool and wood smoke and stinging cold. Fifty yards down the slope, the river, as if aroused by the activity, lapped and gurgled with a life of its own.

Fulwider had not slept well. Every time he had begun to slip off he had fancied some noise easily interpreted as a soft footfall, such as an approaching wolf might make.

It had snowed lightly during the night. He shook the powder off his blanket, rolled it and the rest of his minimal bedding into a compact cylinder the way the old wolfer had demonstrated in town, secured the cover and stepped a few yards away to attend to a basic biological function. When he returned, North and Crippen were hunkered on opposite sides of the fire conversing in gutturals.

"When you figure it was?" the foreman was saying.

"Midnight, maybe. Before the snow." The wolfer used his knife to turn over the bacon, which was hissing and spitting now like a nest of rattlesnakes.

"Wonder what scared them off?"

"Us, I reckon."

Fulwider asked them what they were talking about.

"Come on." Crippen stood and, snatching a flaming stick from the fire, led the easterner beyond its light to a point where the slope flattened out before attempting the climb toward the distant peaks. There he held out the make-shift torch and pointed to a confusion of huge paw prints in the snow. They were half filled with fresh white powder.

Fulwider's heart sprang into his throat. He took an involuntary step backward toward the warmth and security of the fire. "Old tracks?" he stammered hopefully.

"Depends on what you call old." The cowhand's tone was mockingly solemn. "Six hours ain't old to me, but then I been around a lot longer than you."

"While we were sleeping!" Fulwider remembered the noises he had put down to imagination.

"Appears that way."

He retreated another step. "Why? What could they possibly want?"

"Well, I could say our throats, but I don't get the charge I used to out of hoorawing tenderfeet. They wouldn't attack a man if he was standing on the last scrap of meat between them and starvation. I figure it was the fire. They come in for a closer look-see, was all."

"I thought wild animals were afraid of fire."

"That don't mean they don't wonder about them that makes it. Wolves are the curiousest critters on God's good earth. Back in my trapping days I used to snag as many of them with a fancy bandana or a piece of rope for bait as I did with meat and scent. There ain't a lofer living can pass up an interesting piece of junk.''

"Do you think Black Jack was with them?"

"Can't say. These parts are lousy with the bastards.''

"Grub's getting cold," announced North.

Crippen produced plates, cups and utensils of dull metal from his packs and the three sat around the fire munching crisp bacon and scooping up blackened beans in silence, washing everything down with bitter coffee poured steaming from a pot that had been keeping warm on the edge of the fire. As he ate, North had a queer, dog-like habit of glancing around agitatedly, as if wary that someone or something was lurking nearby to snatch away his meal. But for that, he and the foreman appeared indifferent to the fare itself. To Fulwider, who had been too weary and too distracted by the wolves' howling to take much notice of last night's meal, breakfast was even better than the stew he had devoured in the restaurant in town.

It did not occur to him until he was scrubbing the dishes in the swift, cold water of the river that this was the first morning in months he had not awakened with an overpowering urge to cough, or the consequent desire to subdue it with liquor. Perhaps, he mused, the secret was to rise ahead of the malady.

The sun had not yet risen when they broke camp. In spite of the cold, the river crossing went better than Fulwider had feared upon observing the waters swollen from the thaw in the high altitudes and great jagged chunks of ice racing past the steep banks. His pack horse stumbled in mid-stream, but amid shouts from North and Crippen to keep taut the lead line he managed to help the beast regain its footing and reach the other side without further incident. From there they followed a furrowing path identified by Crippen as an old elk run in the direction of the lake.

Snow exploded in front of them and something brownish gray bounded out of the rut and up the soaring incline to their left, its limbs stretching almost parallel to the rocky surface as it climbed with uncanny swiftness toward the summit. The foreman's rifle crashed. The magnificent flying form crumpled suddenly and rolled, skidding and thrashing, until it lay unmoving in an insignificant heap at the base of the slope. It had a goatlike head and enormous ringed horns that curled in upon themselves like snail shells.

"One dead ram," said Crippen, levering a fresh round into the Henry's chamber. "Ain't often you get a chance at them mountain sheep this far down. After forage, I expect." He poked another cartridge into the magazine.

North regarded him flatly. "You wolf passing strange."

"Preach me no sermons. You know as good as me they're attracted to gunfire."

"That was back in buffalo days, when shots meant meat for the taking. These wolves wasn't born then."

"Black Jack was. He's eight if he's a day."

"I don't hold with vain killing," Fulwider interjected stiffly, "whether it's of man or beast."

Crippen scabbarded the Henry. "When I kill, I kill for good reasons."

"Why? We have sufficient supplies."

Dismounting, the foreman produced a half-pint bottle from a saddle pouch and strode over to the carcass. He squatted and used his boot knife to carve a strip of tallow from the sheep's sleek haunches. This he cut into three sections roughly the size of playing cards, made a slot in each and laid them to one side. He then uncorked the bottle and shook a colorless prism into the palm of his hand. He had placed it inside the slot of the first piece of tallow, molded it into a compact ball, set it aside and was about to repeat the procedure with the second when North struck him.

He was out of his saddle and upon Crippen in three strides. Fulwider heard three rapid blows like a string of firecrackers exploding, and then the older man was stretched out beside the carcass while North picked up the ball of tallow, removed the crystal and dropped it back inside the bottle. He rammed in the cork with the heel of his hand.

The foreman sat up and tested his jaw. Glaring hatred, he gathered his legs beneath him to rise. At sight of the wolfer's knife he checked his momentum and fell back on invective.

"You crazy-mad son of a bitch! What's the matter with you? A poison capsule is the surest way there is of killing wolves!"

"And bear and fox and whatever else happens to come along and help itself to a hunk of fresh-killed mutton," finished the other. There was no anger in his tone, just that dead calm that Fulwider had come to recognize as a dangerous sign. "Worse than that. It's a slow death and wolves get a lot of time to heave and slobber the stuff out on the snow and the ground, and there it stays for ten years or a hundred, no one knows for sure how long. You don't know what might eat it or what might eat him that ate it. Or maybe you like the idea of murdering some hunter's little girl fifty years after you're dead."

North forced the bottle of strychnine crystals into Crippen's hand. "Put that back with your gear. I'd throw it away, except it's only a matter of time before some varmint comes along and claws out the cork. If I see it again I'll kill you."

Stepping around the foreman, he squatted over the kill and began separating hide from muscle with long sure strokes of his utilitarian blade. From the haunches he carved dripping red steaks as thick as a man's wrist. "No sense their going to waste," he muttered as he wrapped them in sections of hide and got up to lash the package onto his pack horse's back.

Crippen got up, brushing morosely at the snow that clung to his trousers. Then he put away the controversial bottle and lent his efforts to the butchering.

While the pair was thus engaged, Fulwider reached into his own saddle pouch and pushed the strychnine he had purchased in Rebellion to the very bottom.

For the rest of the day the extinct game trail led them ever higher along a twisting route between sheer walls of dead gray granite and jet sandstone and curious vertical streaks of brick red, which upon inquiring the journalist learned represented iron ore seepage from above. The walls didn't match at all for several miles, an eerie stretch bordered on one side by multicolored strata and on the other by pinnacles of blinding white chalk, remains of a major fault wedged open by the glacier's relentless advance ten thousand years earlier. Clumps of birch and blue spruce clung stubbornly to the faces here and there where the soil in which they were rooted had snatched hold of narrow ledges after sliding down from the top. Far below, water whumped and boomed angrily inside parallel grottos carved to resemble Roman arches in the limestone base. Fulwider was startled, then enchanted when an otter looked out at him with glossy black eyes from a shallow cave as he passed by within an arm's length.

They camped at sunset in the shelter of a smooth, dish-shaped depression worn by high water into the chalk cliff where they dined on savory mutton and the journalist's own treat, peaches canned in their own juice. While North consumed his portion with customary lack of interest, Crippen forgot his disgruntlement over the morning's confrontation and dug in with an energy that made Fulwider fear for the can.

That night it was North who had trouble resting. Fulwider was dimly aware of him writhing all night under his blanket, muttering oaths in a voice so low he could recognize but a few. Once he shot bolt upright and bellowed a name that tore the others out of their own dreams and echoed down the canyon wall like the laughter of a hundred retreating devils. The fire had died to glowing coals, but in their reddish light the wolfer's expression went from raw terror to bewilderment and finally, as he looked around and met first Fulwider's curious gaze and then Crippen's, sullen defiance. He turned over onto one side and drew the blanket over his shoulder. Presently the even rise and fall of the cover indicated that he had drifted into a deep sleep at last.

The journalist bundled up for what he knew must be a vain effort to follow North's example. True relaxation would be out of the question until he knew who the woman named Leah was who haunted the wolfer's dreams.

# SIX

"R. G., if I didn't know you better I would swear that was a blasphemy I just heard."

Busy loading his pack horse in the surly light of another false dawn, Fulwider refrained from explaining to his bemused friend that blasphemies were to a journalist what a stout rope was to a cowboy. He had been on his best behavior thus far, but the discovery that one of his packs was missing had torn a choice oath from his lips before he'd had time to think. He told Crippen of his plight.

"Must of broke loose in the river." He set his cinch and folded down the latigo. "What was in it?"

"Some extra tins of food, which I can do without. And four boxes of ammunition for my rifle, which I cannot. I didn't miss it until just now."

Crippen stared. "Four *boxes?* How long did you figure to be gone?"

"I am rusty," he said shamefacedly.

"I reckon so. Well, don't fret over it."

"But the only cartridge I have is in my gun."

"Don't fret, I said."

The journalist was still puzzling over these cryptic words of reassurance two hours later, when they drew within sight of a trapper's shack built of sod and huddled into a jagged fissure in the canyon wall. A black man with a blunt face full of coiled white whiskers, red-and-black-checked shirt-sleeves rolled up past his elbows, knelt on the rocky ground in front, toiling over a fresh hide he had staked out in the sun.

A chestnut stallion was saddled nearby, tethered beside a squat burro whose razor back was rounded over with bundles. Both were oblivious to the proximity of five dead wolves of varied sizes hanging tails down from the cabin roof, one of which had been skinned. Fulwider, who had never before seen a wolf alive or dead, was surprised and not a little disappointed to discover that the largest was no bigger than some dogs he had seen strolling with their masters in Central Park. None sported the infamous black mantle, and so he quickly lost interest in them as he watched the trapper at work. His forearms stained crimson, the Negro was rubbing down the stretched hide with a grayish, sponge-like material that oozed red liquid.

"Morning, Esau," greeted Crippen, drawing rein. "Fair catch."

"Done better. Who's your friends?" He spoke without looking up. His voice was a monotonous growl.

The foreman made introductions. Esau grunted.

"North I heared tell of," he said. "Ought to sing out first, Crip. These eyes ain't what they used to was. Come near to blowing out one of your'n when you showed." Without pausing in his labors he slid a brown-barreled rifle out from the space beneath the hide. It was cocked.

"Expecting trouble?"

"Done had my share this trip. That big gray bastard up there spooked old Fred when I was out checking my snares, near busted my neck. I tracked him down and blowed a hole clean through him longwise when he went to do it again. Then I catched them half-breeds skinning one of my catches. Leg was still in the trap, for chrissake. Got the drop on them and shooed them off proper. When I seen three riders just now I figured it was them coming back with help.''

"Which half-breeds?'' Crippen was tense in his saddle.

"You know damn well which half-breeds.''

"I told them what would happen I caught them on Newcastle land again.''

"Reckon it didn't take.''

Crippen chewed thoughtfully. "Seen them in town morning we rode out. They was hauling a decent load. Must of been ten, twelve hides aback that mangy pack horse of theirs.''

"They had that many, you can bet more'n one wolfer's trap come up empty.''

The silence stretched taut. Fulwider changed the subject. "What's that you're using to cure that hide?'' he inquired of the trapper.

"Brains.''

"Appears you're pulling out.'' The foreman had overcome his dark humor.

"Damn right. I'll have them other hides yanked by noon and then my season's over. Nights get colder when you pass sixty. I'm thinking I'll take up farming or maybe running cattle. This here skin goes to a old Nez Perce who'll be along any time. He done me a turn or two.''

"I'd give my left nut to see you behind a plow,'' chortled Crippen. "That'd be worth writing home about.''

Talk of writing drew Fulwider back to the purpose of his mission. "How long have you been wolfing?''

"I don't,'' said Esau.

"You don't?'' the journalist glanced confusedly at the shaggy gray carcasses suspended from the roof.

"I'm a trapper. There's a difference. Wolves is just one more thing I trap from time to time."

"Balls," Crippen growled. "You never trapped nothing but wolves in your life. You just don't want no one calling you wolfer. I know a rancher like you down below Hell's Canyon. He runs about six cows and five thousand sheep. But he calls himself a cattleman."

Esau said nothing. The gray matter in his hands made wet swiping sounds against the underside of the stretched pelt. "What you want?" he asked at length.

"City feller here needs cartridges for a 50-70 Remington. Got any?"

"In the cabin." He rose without looking at any of his visitors, tossed the crushed handful of brains onto the hide and shambled, splay-footed, through the low door of the sod hut. Five minutes crawled past. North made a noise of impatience. The black man returned, carrying a leather sack the size of a melon. "Let's see your hands."

Fulwider hesitated, then complied, extending them backs up as he had in grammar school for fingernail inspection. The trapper snorted impatiently and turned them over to view the palms.

"Medium. Dollar a handful." He held out the open sack, inside of which glittered a mound of brass cartridges.

"A dollar!" the journalist exclaimed. "I never heard of such a price!"

"Don't like it, go next door."

"Pay the man," Crippen directed.

Fulwider slapped a silver dollar into the man's free hand and helped himself to as many shells as he could gather in one spread palm. The sack was immediately withdrawn.

"Seen Black Jack lately?" asked the foreman.

"Don't see him hanging there, do you?" Esau put down the sack, sank to his knees and picked up the bloody matter once again. It squished over the skin's tawny surface.

"Black bastard," ground out Crippen, after they had passed beyond earshot of the cabin. "I would of sent him packing ten years ago if Old Man Meredith and him wasn't such good buddies. He does kill wolves, though. I bet he has a couple of hunnert dollars' worth of skins in that there shack. And that's one more thing that bothers me about him."

"I don't see why it should," said Fulwider. "Isn't that what you want him to do? Kill wolves?"

"Trouble is he brings in just as many hides whether the picking is high or low. He ain't that good and no one is that lucky. I suspect he raises the critters for the bounty. If I could find out where he does it I would skin him myself."

"That's barbaric!"

"Hell no, it's common. There's different ways of doing it. Most wolfers don't kill bitches on account of they are the ones have the litters. That would be like shooting the paymaster. Some take it a step farther and raise them theirselves, just like cattle or horses. When the litters get big enough they poison their feed. It's steady income and the Idaho Stockmen's Association don't ask questions so long as the hides and scalps keep coming in."

"Astonishing. But doesn't that defeat the purpose of the bounty?"

"Wolfers don't treat with purposes. They're in it for the money. You see now why no self-respecting cattleman will sit down and have a drink with one?"

As he spoke, his eyes were on Asa North. But the latter appeared too intent upon studying the snowy ground at his roan's feet to have heard.

The trail leveled off a mile south of the trapper's cabin, at which point signs of their quarry began to appear in the form of more tracks and an occasional swirl of bloody slush where a mole or fieldmouse had ventured improvidently from its snug burrow and been snapped up for its audacity. The first time they came upon evidence of such a Liliputian drama, Fulwider was surprised and asked if these could be the same predators that had been slaughtering Meredith's cattle.

"They ain't particular," replied Crippen. "You got to remember that wolves spend ninety percent of their time looking for food. You go without eating six days at a stretch and see if you don't develop a taste for mouse."

The journalist had much to be grateful for in Crippen. Given North's taciturn nature, if not for the foreman Fulwider would remain as ignorant of the animal they sought as he had been at the journey's outset. It was he who explained, when the wolfer would not, that the reason they scanned the sky while tracking was to note the direction in which the ravens were flying. Carrion-eaters were known to follow wolves in anticipation of a feast, much as gulls flocked around whales to feed on the parasites that infested their hides.

But enthralled though the easterner was with these gratuitous insights, Asa North fascinated him even more. He rode with his rifle across the throat of his saddle, carried no other weapon save the skinning knife and for all the years he must have spent on horseback he did not ride particularly well. Whenever the opportunity arose he would abandon the creature and strike off on foot to read a sign or determine the wind's direction. The horse sensed this and seldom missed a chance to cause its rider discomfort. Yet they looked after each other during harrowing moments with the faithfulness of the mutually dependent. The relationship between North and Crippen was drawn along similar lines.

Fulwider was contemplating his unenviable role as buffer

between two volatile personalities when the trio topped a rise overlooking four rust-colored hulks lying a hundred yards apart in a field of trampled snow.

The cattle might have been asleep but for the blood that smeared the scene in crimson streaks and whorls of pale pink and darkened the creatures' hides where it no longer flowed. A funereal silence settled over the riders as they stopped to take it in.

"Goddamn," said Crippen. "Goddamn." He dug in his spurs and the sorrel shot forward, jerking his gray in its wake. North and the journalist followed.

As they drew near, a gray head came up on the other side of the near carcass, lingered long enough for Fulwider to observe its scarlet muzzle, then dropped from sight and a fleet from dashed toward a nearby stand of firs.

Crippen's horse, out in front, came to a skidding stop as the foreman leaned back on the reins and clawed the Henry out of its scabbard. But North's roan was slower to react to its master's hand and drew abreast, inadvertently blocking Crippen's line of fire just as he was shouldering the weapon. Meanwhile Fulwider, still gathering momentum when the wolf had appeared, slowed to a halt and drew the Remington from his bedroll, taking aim even as North sighted in his Ballard. The weapons double-crashed in the crisp mountain air.

The wolf yelped, a terrible bellow of rage and pain, executed a hurtling triple somersault and came to a rest in the shade of the trees whose shelter it had sought.

The rifle's recoil had left Fulwider's shoulder numb. When he had satisfied himself that nothing was broken, he threw the gun across his pommel and rode over to join the others at the firs. The animal was still alive and struggling to rise despite the blood that covered its haunches. To the journalist's report-deadened ears its whimpers and whines were scarcely audible.

"He's yours, Mr. Newspaper Writer," North said. "Finish him."

"I think it was your bullet that hit him."

Crippen shook his head. "He missed. His horse was still moving when he shot. No thirty-eight punched that hole in its spine. You best get to it while we still got horses."

The smells of blood and wolf were making the mounts dance and shy. Fulwider stepped down and reloaded. The predator had ceased its struggles and lay panting on its side, one brown eye following the movements of its assailant. Leaning down, the easterner placed the muzzle behind the beast's ear and squeezed the trigger. The report seemed twice as loud as that which had preceded it. The wolf threw up its smashed head and sprawled back down in the dark red snow.

Lifeless, it appeared much smaller than when first encountered. Crippen stooped to pull back a rubbery lip with his thumb, exposing an incarnadined tongue clamped between curving yellow fangs. Some teeth were missing, and most that remained had been worn down to pyramidal nubs. The gums were stained vermilion. He straightened.

"Old. At least ten years. Loner, likely, following the pack." He handed Fulwider his knife. "Just the scalp. Furriers will give you another five for the hide, but we got bigger game to chase."

"I'd rather not." Fulwider extended the knife for him to take back.

The foreman's expression hardened. "You kill, you cut. Don't never ask no one to do your job."

"It's all right. I'll forfeit the bounty."

Crippen made no move to accept the blade. The wind freshened, drawing his collar across the lower part of his face so that only his eyes were exposed, fixed and humorless. North broke the spell.

"Don't," he told the journalist, "yelp."

He spaced out the words like separate sentences. Under his flat scrutiny, Fulwider withdrew the knife and crouched over the slain wolf.

Its coat felt warm to the touch. Lying on its side that way, it reminded him so much of a sleeping dog in spite of the pulpy mess he had made of its head that he was reluctant to make the first cut for fear it would cry out. Crippen mistook his hesitation for ignorance of how to begin and guided the hand grasping the knife with his own, describing a phantom incision clear around the animal's head under the ears. He let go and stood back to supervise.

North, who had spent much of this time pacing back and forth, lost patience suddenly and shouldered the journalist aside just as he had begun sawing at the tough membrane. In less time than it takes to describe it, the wolfer scored his blade around the mutilated skull and peeled the scalp from the bone with a nasty sucking noise. Straightening, he thrust the bloody relic at Fulwider, who ignored it.

"I suppose we split the bounty," declared the other stiffly.

"What's yours stays yours." North cast the scalp at Fulwider's feet, plunged his knife into the snow and scraped the blade clean on a patch of exposed dead grass. "You was just taking too much time about it."

"Take it," Crippen advised. "If you don't, someone else will. Maybe Fire Eye and Lightfoot."

He obeyed moodily, folding the gory surface inside and tucking it into his saddle pouch.

The cattle slaughtered by the predators lay on their sides and stomachs, heads twisted so that the five-foot horns for which the breed was named stuck up in the air like crooked flagstaffs. They included two elderly cows and a half-grown calf run to ground after a chase, according to the tracks, of less than a thousand feet, and a large bull whose many grisly wounds bespoke a costly victory on the part of its tormentors. For two hundred yards around its massive remains there wasn't a square inch of earth that hadn't been torn by its slashing hoofs. All of the victims had been pulled down by the shoulders and their intestines devoured.

Further investigation uncovered the mangled remains of what North identified as a male yearling wolf in a blackberry bramble more than a hundred yards from the point where the hunters had caught up with the bull. No tracks led up to it, and it was determined that the beast had been hurled there on the horns of the besieged herd leader. Crippen claimed the scalp as the man who had made the discovery.

"Dawn, maybe a little later." The foreman swung into saddle. "They know someone's after them or they wouldn't of left so much meat behind."

Mounting, North nodded. "They'll be taking to the high ground here on out." He urged the roan forward.

Crippen turned a grim face on the journalist. "Going to write about this here?"

"If I can find the words," he confirmed. "It's one thing to quote statistics about how much livestock is destroyed annually, but the impact of first-hand evidence is so much greater."

"It's like coming home and finding your daughter raped," said the foreman, and moved out into the wolfer's path.

## SEVEN

For two days the trail they were following wound steadily upward, where nature knew no rounded edges and breathing the air was like inhaling needles. They had passed the thaw belt the first day and were moving deeper into the region where spring never visited. There were places where the riders had to dismount and literally drag their horses, digging in their hoofs and whinnying, one by one up steep inclines while the reins slashed their gloves to ribbons and rubbed the flesh from their palms. The jagged scenery resembled nothing in Fulwider's experience, and even when, after acres of dead white, they moved into tall stands of evergreens spaced like whiskers on a Chinaman's chin, he felt as out of place as a visitor to Monsieur Verne's moon.

Many wolf tracks spotted their path. Once, when they came upon evidence of an unsuccessful chase involving the pack and a number of mountain sheep that ended when the intended prey took to the peaks, Fulwider commented that the pack must be growing desperate after two days without feeding. Crippen dismissed this, explaining that the stomach of a full-grown wolf could hold as much as sixty pounds, enough to see it through five days of fasting. When the journalist expressed disbelief, North astonished them both by declaring that it was more like two hundred pounds, and that they could go without food for nearly two weeks. Pressed for further information, however, he fell back on his usual grunting responses.

The New Yorker was losing patience with the man he had come along to write about. Time and again he had attempted to smash through North's hostile barrier and had met only rebuff. The situation was especially intolerable in view of his certainty that the wolfer had much to offer that Crippen could not. More and more, Fulwider found his thoughts returning to his friend's assertion that North's success in wolfing was related to his having become one himself.

Late in the morning of the third day after encountering the slain cattle, they picked their way up a craggy precipice and found themselves on the edge of a level expanse that stretched for a snowswept quarter of a mile before climbing to the highest peaks in the range. There they paused. For a moment the journalist was at a loss to understand why, or what it was that had drawn his partners' attention. Then he spotted a line of shapes towing a cloud of snow across the base of the soaring rocks. These he took to be a herd of elk moving swiftly, but not nearly as swiftly as a column of much smaller forms circling around to head them off from the south. The creature at the head of the column was a smear of black and gray, and in the gray phalanx behind followed another that was almost pure white.

# EIGHT

The scene was five hundred yards off, beyond effective range of even the Remington. The three watched helplessly as it unfolded, North in silence, Crippen chewing agitatedly, Fulwider in dumb, morbid fascination as the predators swung inexorably around in a semicircle from the rear to close in on the stragglers falling behind the fleeing herd. It was a wonderfully precise maneuver that put the journalist in mind of diagrams he had seen of famous European battles. Napoleon's army had marched with no greater purpose to divide the massed forces of Russia and Austria at Austerlitz.

He counted thirteen wolves strung out nose to tail, heads thrust forward in line with their spines while their tails described horizontal slashes behind so that they resembled nothing so much as a succession of arrows directed one after the other toward a single target. Ankles flicking beneath, they were making incredible speed with no apparent effort, and when the big wolf up front drew abreast of a young elk, closed its jaws on the beast's shaggy right shoulder and dragged it to earth beneath its own forward momentum within a hundred yards, the deed seemed almost casual.

But the victim was much the stronger of the two. It was on its feet again after a brief struggle and plunging to narrow the gap between itself and the protection of the herd. The wolf hung on, however, letting its limbs drag and using them only to avoid injury when the antelope-like creature slashed at it with its near hind hoof. Meanwhile the dangerous gap widened, and the other wolves leaped and tore at their prey's flanks. Blood spattered the snow. The elk stumbled, rose and stumbled again, and before it could thrash upright a third time it was aswarm with heaving gray bodies. Abruptly its struggles ended.

The remainder of the herd had not slackened its pace in the meantime, and though four or five wolves made feints at the retreating host it was plain that they were only engaging in sport, and as they fell back to join the feast the elk stampeded over a ridge and out of sight.

Crippen gave his reins a snap, but North lunged and grasped the sorrel's bit chain before it could break into gallop. It snorted in confusion.

"Where I growed up it's considered mighty unfriendly to take control of another man's horse," snarled the foreman, over his drawn Colt.

North said, "Let them feed. When they get their bellies full they won't be in any shape to run."

Their gazes locked. At length the wolfer released Crippen's mount and the gun was returned to its holster.

"Next time say something first."

They dismounted to rest the horses. For two hours they watched as the hunting creatures gorged themselves on warm meat and lapped at the bloodstained snow. Some finished early and wandered away, nipping at each other playfully like children at a picnic, while others stretched out in pillowy drifts to sleep and digest. Fights broke out occasionally among those feeding, but these invariably ended with one of the combatants rolling onto its back in a signal of surrender rather than continuing to the death, as the journalist had anticipated. He saw nothing of the dark-mantled male after the kill but assumed he was among those on the other side of the carcass. From time to time he spotted the white female walking around among the others as if to ensure that none claimed more than its share. It was a pastoral scene, all the more so because of the violent one that had preceded it.

North swung a leg over the roan. "We'll circle in from the north, upwind."

They approached at a walk. With the wind in their faces they escaped the animals' notice until the distance had closed by two thirds, where they stepped down and sank into a crouch. From here they could see the dead elk's great rib cage, hung with strips of hide and sinew. Wolves lay and sat around it licking their chops and gazing around with sleepy, sated looks on their incredibly doglike faces. There was still no sign of the leader.

Crippen tugged at Fulwider's sleeve.

"See to your horses," he whispered. "Hang on hard to their noses and mind they don't snort nor whinny. They ain't trained wolfers and if they get a whiff of them black-hearted bastards we won't get so much as a hair."

"But how will I fire my rifle?"

"You won't. You're here for a story, remember? Not bounty. That lofer you shot was a lucky bonus."

At that moment the wolfer's Ballard spoke. Two hundred yards away a rangy male with a white ruff encircling its neck half reared and fell where it had been sitting atop a snowy bank. In a flash North reloaded and fired again, and yet again. Two more wolves dropped. One, though dark at the shoulder, wasn't big enough to fit Black Jack's official

description. The second was even smaller and evidently female.

Dale Crippen, caught by surprise, unlimbered his repeater and hammered three times rapidly at the predators.
But by this time the pack had scattered, and through the
confusion and scudding black-powder smoke Fulwider was
unable to see the result. He glimpsed a large gray shape
darting from behind the slain elk and over the far ridge. A
similar shape, pure white, followed hard on its heels.

The reports echoed sizzling in the distance. In the stillness afterward, five gray carcasses lay about the torn hulk.

"You missed some," commented North, reloading.

"I didn't have your head start." The foreman punched
shells into his magazine with a savage thumb.

"That white-ruffed male was looking right at me. You
two appeared to be busy, so I started without you. I thought
maybe Jack would be first from behind the elk when the
shooting started. He wasn't."

He got to his feet with a quick, animal-like pounce and,
grasping the roan's bridle, started on foot toward the death
scene. The black tethered behind followed docilely.

"I believe all that," Crippen rejoined, leading his own
pair. "Yes, sir, Mr. Living Legend. I believe all that."

Although flat in appearance, the landscape was really a
series of moraines rounded by erosion and snow, and as
the hunters descended into a horizontal trough more than a
mile long, the ridge in front of them obscured the killing
ground. By the time they surmounted it they found they
were no longer alone.

The slight figure in the battered round hat and buffalo
coat had his back to them as he bent over the wolf with
the white ruff. Crippen clanked the Henry's lever, causing
him to turn. He had a scarlet-stained skinning knife in his

left hand with which he had slit the dead wolf's pelt from throat to belly.

"Still rustling, Sam?" The foreman had the rifle braced against his hip on a level with the half-breed's head.

Sam Fire Eye smiled. He had sleepy, insolent eyes behind the spectacles, and his narrow face was so scarred by smallpox that his days-old whiskers straggled out between the pits like grass in a quarry.

"Hell," he drawled, his voice a nasal tenor, "you know the rule. First hand on the kill is the hand that gets it."

"Not anymore it ain't. Not for forty years. Now it's the hand that jerks the trigger." For emphasis he wriggled his finger on the trigger of the rifle. "Where's Dick?"

Iron teeth shone dully in Fire Eye's grin. "Behind you."

The foreman chewed thoughtfully. His eyes jumped to Fulwider and then back to the half-breed. "Take a look."

Fulwider looked. The man with the tall hat and long black hair was standing atop the ridge over which they had just come, a Sharps carbine cradled in his hands. He wore a sheepskin vest over a blue flannel shirt and leggings, and the lack of emotion in his obsidian eyes chilled the journalist to the marrow. He informed Crippen of the situation.

North watched Fire Eye and said nothing.

"Reckon we walked into it this time," sighed the foreman.

"That'd be a fair description." Sam straightened. "We figured Black Jack would head up here with you fellows dogging him. We was in town for provisions Tuesday, and when we seen you heading out we knowed who you'd be after. Figured maybe we could head you off and have us some sport."

"For the fifty bucks these here skins will bring you? You come mighty cheap, Sam."

The grin died. "It ain't the money! It's last November

and a gristly old bastard that run us off so's he could have
Jack all to hisself. Wasn't for you, we'd of collected that
six hunnert last year."

"Excuse me all to hell. You are a higher-priced son of
a bitch than I give you credit for."

"And you're stupider than I thought, talking like that
with a Big Fifty on your back. Now, give me them weapons." He took a step forward with his right hand outstretched.

"I reckon not."

At North's words the half-breed stopped. The Ballard
was pointing at his belt buckle.

"You're Asa North, ain't you?" Fire Eye said. The ghost
of his former smile pulled at the corners of his mouth. "I
seen you once in Helena, toting that big old wolf they had
a two-hunnert-dollar bounty on. Old Three Toes. I was just
getting set to light out after him myself. Yes, sir, you must
of been something in them days. Shoot him, Dick."

North flung himself to the ground at the very instant the
Sharps roared behind him. He struck on his elbow and fired.
Sam Fire Eye cried out and spun, clapping his knife hand
to his right shoulder. Crippen began shooting then, working
the trigger as rapidly as he could lever in fresh rounds. Fire
Eye's helpless body danced as the bullets found their mark.

There was a loud thump as of an axe sinking into soft
wood. Crippen arched his back and folded forward, first to
his knees and then onto his face, still clutching the Henry.
The handle of a knife twanged between his shoulder blades.

North was busy reloading. Fulwider whirled to see Dick
Lightfoot, who had hurled the knife, hastily poking a new
cartridge into the single-shot Sharps. The journalist lunged
and tore his Remington free of his bedroll, yanking the
trigger even as Lightfoot raised the carbine. He missed, but

the bullet whining past the half-breed's ear threw off his aim and he fired high over Fulwider's head.

The wolfer shouldered his Ballard, but Lightfoot's paint was close by—he got a leg up and was over the ridge in a flurry of hoofs and snow. North's bullet tore off his hat just as he dropped from sight.

Blue smoke crawled across the suddenly still field of battle. Sam Fire Eye lay on his back in the snow, arms at his sides and spread slightly, his pale shirtfront mottled red where the coat was unbuttoned. His derby was tilted over his forehead at a rakish angle. Six feet away, Dale Crippen was stretched motionless across his rifle, scarlet seepage glistening around the hilt of the knife in his back.

Fulwider knelt beside him and turned the foreman's head gently so that he could place his ear next to his friend's lips. After a moment of intense listening, he picked up a very faint whisper of breath fluttering in and out. Gingerly he touched the knife's leatherbound handle.

"Leave it in!"

The journalist started and snatched up his rifle, only to relax when he recognized North standing over him. He hadn't heard him approaching.

"Right now that blade's the only thing that's keeping him from bleeding to death," the wolfer explained.

"What should we do?" Fulwider's throat felt constricted.

"What we should do is leave him here. He ain't going to make it." He was breathing heavily. "Give me a hand with him."

Getting Crippen's one hundred and seventy pounds of sinew over his horse's back without killing him in the process was the hardest work the man from New York had ever known. Wheezing and swaying under his half of the burden, he steadied the nervous beast with one hand while the wolfer heaved the limp body across the saddle. With a length of rope they secured his wrists and ankles beneath the mare's belly. North was setting the knot when Fulwider noticed a spreading stain on the wolfer's buckskin shirt near his ribs.

"You're hit!"

"Grazed by the Sharps. It's a scratch." He stepped away from the horse, staggered and almost fell.

"Let me see."

The other raised his shirt to reveal a crimson gash four inches long on his left side just above the belt. It had bled considerably.

Fulwider told him to take off his wolfskin and shirt. When he obeyed, the journalist cleansed the wound with water from his canteen, fashioned a pad bandage from his own shirttail and anchored it in place with more gingham strips wound twice around the wolfer's abdomen with a loop over his shoulder to keep them from slipping. North flinched when the blood was sponged off but didn't cry out.

While his partner dressed, the man from New York removed the bundles from his and Crippen's pack horses, discarded them and turned the animals loose, keeping only North's black, whose reins he wrapped around the horn of his own saddle. North nodded in weak approval. The extra responsibility would only slow them down, and they wouldn't need as many supplies for the journey back anyway. From that point on, Fulwider was in charge.

# NINE

In years to come he would remember the trek back to town as one of those nightmares that seem always to have reached their bleakest depth, then get worse. Because he was ignorant of the shorter route the half-breed had used, Fulwider was forced to return over the same ground while his trailwise partner, the blood soaking through his bandage and down his pants leg, floated on the edge of cooperation and expended most of his energy trying to remain upright in the saddle. In this manner the days and nights passed in a confusing blur of black and white without tally.

They made it back to the trapper's shack without stopping except to remove the semiconscious Crippen from his horse when the pain grew too great and to eat and sleep in snatches while the horses rested. They built no fires, subsisting on squares of salt pork carved from North's meager stores and slaking their thirst with melted snow forced by the handful into their canteens. Fulwider was nearly lost when his gray missed its footing on the narrow ledge two hundred feet above the river, but the pack horse leaned back on its haunches and held the lead line taut until balance was achieved.

"Next time lean out," barked North, enjoying a lucid

moment. "When you lean in you throw his feet over the edge."

In the shack, abandoned now and smelling of old hides, the journalist changed Crippen's bandage, a wad of gingham rudely stuffed into the wound once the knife had finally been removed. The wound was too clean. The foreman was bleeding internally, but there was nothing he or anyone else but a trained physician could do about it. Next he turned his attention to North's injury. He was concerned by the color of the puckered flesh around the gash, and used the wolfer's own blade to trim away the discolored fringe. Fulwider might have been altering his sleeve for all the reaction he got. They rested there two hours and were moving again before sunup.

When North's bleeding had stopped he had shown signs of recovering from his weakness, but as they moved closer to the river his condition worsened. At first Fulwider put it down to exhaustion, and read little into the other's slumped posture that he didn't share. At length he halted to inquire after him, placing a hand on the roan's neck to check its movement. The wolfer immediately slid from his saddle. Fulwider caught him in both arms and with his last ounce of strength pushed him back into precarious balance astride the skittish mount. He then got down to examine him.

He smelled the rotting flesh even before the wound was bared in all its ghastly putrescence. This was the first time he had encountered gangrene firsthand.

This was a dilemma. In his research into the West he had come upon many tales in which festering wounds had been treated with searing knives or red-hot pokers, but in North's condition he wasn't at all sure that such a remedy wouldn't kill him from shock. In addition, the time consumed in building a fire, treating and rebandaging the wound could be fatal to Crippen, for whom each hour of delay was a fresh nail in his coffin. He had no choice but to keep moving and pray for the best.

At the river, Fulwider turned loose the last pack horse and took Crippen across first aback the mare, leading it by the reins. Then he came back for North, whose hands he had lashed to the saddle horn to prevent his falling. He was too tired to return for the black and left it behind.

The wolfer was babbling deliriously by the time they reached town long after nightfall. Over and over he repeated the name "Leah," and words in a guttural language that heid no meaning for his partner even had he strength enough to listen. He dismounted in front of the steps that led up to the doctor's office over the general merchandise, where a crowd was gathering around the horses. His knees gave out then, and he sank as through water to the muddy surface of the street.

"It's that journalist feller," announced a voice on the other side of a dream.

"Who's that with him?" asked another.

"Jesus Christ, it's Asa North!"

"He's alive, I think."

"They was hauling a dead man."

"It looks like Dale Crippen!"

Fulwider lost his purchase on reality at that point and plunged into a swirling void.

## TEN

Following an inquest based on information supplied by R. G. Fulwider and sworn to in the presence of Sheriff Oscar Adamson, Dale Crippen was declared dead "of an injury inflicted upon him by a person known to this court" and buried with all due ceremony at Newcastle Ranch. Neither of the men who had accompanied him on his last hunt were in attendance, Fulwider suffering from exhaustion and consumptive relapse, Asa North recuperating from treatment for gangrene.

Dr. Gedalia Earthman, a young practitioner of limited experience, had at first despaired of the wolfer's life. Immediately upon admitting him to his office he had worked swiftly to pare away the mortified flesh and cauterized the wound, but by then the poison had entered the patient's bloodstream. The doctor devoted most of his time to treating Fulwider, for whom there was far greater cause to hope, and waited for the inevitable.

No one was more surprised than he when, on the fourth day of North's illness, the fever broke and he was heard to call for his clothes and rifle. Hours later he was pronounced on his way toward total recovery. Earthman had heard of nothing like it, and wrote to one of his former medical professors to inquire if he should present the facts in the form of a paper to a national journal.

Meanwhile, North was held for observation until early April, when upon his return after delivering a baby out of town, the physician found the cot in his office deserted. Subsequent investigation revealed that the patient had settled his bill at the hotel and livery, collected his horse, purchased provisions enough for ten days' journey and vanished. Earthman found more money than was owed him stuffed into a beaker on his instrument shelf.

The wolfing season was on the wane by this time, and after the first rush of homesteaders and cattlemen had plundered the stores of spring necessities, Rebellion sank back into its soporific routine. Fulwider spent much of that period convalescing in his hotel room under the care of kindly Mrs. Earthman. A pleasant plump lady of German extraction, she kept the door to the hallway decorously open during her visits, and though she knew precious little English she made the journalist's life a torment by reminding him how much he had given up when he swore off feminine companionship.

His bleak mood didn't improve when a wire arrived from his editor in New York asking if he would mind sharing his experiences from beyond the grave with his many eager readers. Which churlish comment he took to mean that the *World* had grown weary of financing his stay without a single dispatch to show for its investment. Painfully, for his grief over Crippen's loss hung like a great weight from his heart, he called for paper and ink and would have completed a draft of his experiences in the mountains in one day of fevered scribbling had not *Frau* Earthman forcibly removed the pen from his fingers and made him rest after six hours. Under her eagle eye he paced himself over the next two days and sealed the results in an envelope for her to send off via the next mail packet east.

Three days later, he came awake with a start from a recurring nightmare in which he was both the man leading and the corpse draped over a nervous horse on a ledge hundreds of feet above a freezing river. Cold gray light sifted through the east window, making his surroundings seem less solid than the glaring white wall of the canyon from which reality had plucked him. He blinked around stupidly, then cast aside the heavy counterpane and padded barefoot in his nightshirt across the cold floor to peer out through the clouded glass.

His first, irrational thought as he saw the dawn procession approaching was of the notorious western lynch mobs he had read about. But as the crowd drew near the hotel he saw the leaders and abandoned that impression. Two men in clothes of an indescribable filth were carrying the carcass of a wolf up the street, slung from a pole whose ends rested on their shoulders. His initial belief that it was Black Jack fled as the diffused light took on a hard edge and he recognized it as a female, with a blue-gray coat like fogged steel and all its teeth bared in a ghastly, unnatural grin that swayed upside-down with the movement of the dangling head. Its mammaries stood out dark through the thin growth on its underside. All four ankles had been pierced and lashed with thongs to the pole, which had been fashioned from a stout tree limb.

The man in front, smeared like his partner from head to foot with blood and old entrails, was thick-waisted, heavy in the shoulders, and had ugly features under a battered slouch hat. His partner was younger, not as stout, and though he wore a yellow walrus moustache the family resemblance was clear. With a shock the journalist recognized them as the pair North had confronted in Bismarck the day Crippen and he had stopped there. Aaron, the heavy one, appeared to have recovered quite nicely from his knife wound.

They were abreast of the hotel when Oscar Adamson, a fat Swede wearing a hammered brass star on a canvas coat buttoned only at the neck, pried his way through the press of curiosity seekers with a sawed-off shotgun. His clean-shaven face was the color of raw horse meat, a delicacy back east during the Panic of 1873.

"Stemmer, what in hell do you think you are doing?" He placed his bulk squarely in front of the leader. "Do you want me to haul you in for disturbing the peace?"

Aaron grinned wickedly and stepped around him. The crowd surged past the stolid figure of the sheriff, leaving him standing foolishly in the middle of the street with his shotgun nuzzling the ground.

Stopping before the Assiniboin, the men bearing the limb and its burden heaved it away in one smooth motion. The carcass, stiff as a rocking horse, plopped into the mud next to the porch and toppled halfway over onto its back. Some of the people watching stepped backward nervously, as if the beast might yet find life enough to snap at them.

"Got your knife and fork ready, Meredith?" Aaron challenged, shouting at the top of his lungs. He was staring up at Fulwider's floor.

The journalist threw up the sash. Leaning out, he saw the rancher seated half on a sill two windows down. The Englishman was fully dressed in a dark gray suit that clung to his square frame the way the foil wrapper fit the cigar he was industriously peeling.

"What are you babbling about now, Stemmer?" He struck a match on the scaled paint of the window casing and held it beneath the cigar, revolving the latter as he did so to ignite it evenly.

"You don't crawl out of it that easy," replied the man in the street. "You told me on this here spot two months ago that if I ever brung in a bitch wolf weighing more than eighty pounds you'd eat it. I come to see you make good on the bet."

"I see. You have weighed it, then?"

Aaron favored him with his lopsided grin. "All right, if you got to have your nose rubbed in it I'll see you at Grierson's in five minutes. Bring salt and pepper."

Meredith raised a hand and withdrew. A moment later the window came down with a dull thud.

Dressing hurriedly, Fulwider was surprised to learn how much weight he had lost. He was forced to take his belt in three notches, and even then his trousers, tailored especially for his frame, bagged comically in the seat. He studied his reflection while shaving and wondered that he hadn't noticed how big his eyes were getting, or the way the bones stood out in his face.

The entrance of the butcher's shop could only accommodate a fraction of the crowd. Fulwider was fortunate enough to obtain space near the doorway, but those who arrived behind him had to make do with the yellowed windows. Inside, the rank odor of death was a distinct personality, and reminded the journalist sadly of Asa North, who hadn't bothered to tell him goodbye before leaving.

Grierson, the butcher, was a chunky fellow of indeterminate age with a brilliant bald head and an expression fixed in a perennial smile of good will, counterbalanced by an enormous right arm developed through years of slinging around hogs and sides of beef three times his weight. He had a huge balance scale suspended by a chain from the ceiling and operated by means of sandbags in various denominations. This he agreed to use in settling the dispute, after first sizing up the evidence and cutting himself in on the wolfer's side.

A general hubbub greeted the rancher's arrival. He looked tired under his broad-brimmed gray hat, and swung his gold-headed walking stick impatiently when the crowd was slow in clearing a path for him. Angry mutters followed him. Meredith was far from popular in a town whose citizenry was constructed largely of people whose nationalities had known little but suffering at the hands of the British. Two lanky cowhands packing side arms came in behind him and slouched against the wall on either side of the door with thumbs hooked inside brass belt buckles.

"I want it understood that if it weighs less than eighty pounds you will eat it yourself," the Englishman declared.

Aaron Stemmer smirked. "Understood. Look at that frame. She's ninety if she's a pound."

"If she's even seventy I'll help you eat her. Go ahead." He nodded at Grierson.

The butcher started with five twenty-pound sacks on one side of the scale. The man with the yellow moustache, whom Fulwider remembered as Jim, helped him hoist the gray carcass into the other pan and stepped back. Immediately the pan with the sacks sank two feet. Grierson removed one of the sacks. The sides seesawed for an anxious moment, then settled with the sacks still hanging below the slain wolf.

"It ain't eighty," he announced, in a surprised tone.

A murmur rippled through the spectators. Meredith said, "Keep going. We haven't determined yet whether I'll be dining with Stemmer."

For five minutes the butcher worked up a sweat removing and replacing sacks of different weights, grunting when one side or the other dipped below its mate. His smile was an early casualty. Finally he discarded a ten-pound sack and put two smaller bags of different sizes in its place. The pans shifted up and down and swayed to a perfect balance.

"Sixty-seven and a half."

A heavy wagon rumbled past outside, louder than anything in the shop. It was Aaron Stemmer who broke the spell.

"Damn it, Grierson, your scale is busted."

"Like hell it is!" snarled the butcher. "And even if it was, I sure as hell wouldn't leave it reading low."

"They're never as heavy as they look." Meredith's smile was blade-thin. "You know the wager, Stemmer. Chris, cut him off a good-size piece to start."

One of the cowhands produced a knife and stepped up to the carcass. Gripping it by a foreleg, he started sawing at the tender flesh beneath the appendage.

"I won't do it." Aaron backed away, a hunted look on his blunt features. "Wolf meat is tainted."

"You will do it."

The declaration came from behind Fulwider, where Oscar Adamson had stood unnoticed until that moment, holding his shotgun in both hands. His scarlet face was grim.

"I have scraped up too many welshers from too many barroom floors to let it happen here. You made a bet and, goddamn it, I am going to see you pay it off if it means loading this here scattergun with wolf meat and blowing it down your gullet. Eat!"

"I scraped the hair off it for you." The cowboy named Chris thrust a bloody portion skewered on the end of his knife under Aaron's shapeless nose.

For a long time he stared at it. Then his eyes scoured the room restlessly, lighting on Meredith, the sheriff, Jim standing helpless on the other side of the second cowhand and finally the impassive, leathern features of Chris. Gingerly he took the raw chunk between thumb and forefinger and, closing his eyes, popped it into his mouth. He wobbled it around and swallowed it whole.

Tears came to his eyes. He clapped a hand to his mouth, gagging.

"Next time go after something worthwhile, like Black Jack." Meredith caught Chris's eye. "See that he eats every last ounce of the sixty-seven and a half pounds."

"That could take a while," said the employee.

"I won't need you before tomorrow morning." He walked out past Fulwider, trailed by the other cowhand. On the boardwalk he stopped and turned around to stare at the journalist.

"Fulwider, is that you? My God, I didn't recognize you! What happened? No, never mind, that's a ridiculous question. Of course I know what happened. How are you?"

The New Yorker replied that he was holding his own, after a fashion.

"You're just the man I want to see. Do you have a moment?"

"It appears that I have nothing but," came the reply, "at least until I hear again from my newspaper."

The Englishman smiled, his face breaking into a mass of creases Fulwider had not noticed on their last meeting. "Would you object to having a drink with a carpetbagger?"

"Mr. Meredith, I'd drink with the devil himself if he were buying," said the other, answering the smile with one he didn't feel.

"You must learn to call me Nelson." He waved away the bodyguard.

## ELEVEN

"You cannot imagine what it means to me to speak with someone whose conversation isn't sprinkled with 'I reckons' and 'much obligeds.' "

Fulwider smiled politely but said nothing. The bartender, a small man with meaty forearms and a pitted nose like J. P. Morgan's, refilled their glasses with cognac and withdrew. The sun was still climbing. The journalist thought that if he wasn't careful the rest of the day would be lost in an alcoholic haze.

"You're probably curious about what happened in Grierson's," said the rancher.

"It's hardly my business."

A smile fluttered and was gone. "Discretion is something else that dies a quick death out here. Aaron Stemmer and his brother Jim are two of the reasons why I find life on the frontier so hard to bear. They've been asking for today's comeuppance for some time."

"I doubt they'll learn anything from it," said the other, and told of the their role in the Bismarck incident. Meredith listened with eyebrows raised.

"Remarkable." He touched his lips to the edge of his glass. "And yet it's not such a coincidence that you should run into them again so soon. Fewer people live this side of the Missouri than in New York City, and they're moving constantly. The Stemmers will do anything for a dollar and frequently visit Rebellion during the wolfing season. Perhaps my standing with the natives will improve after today.''

"They will probably resent you even more."

The rancher sighed. "I don't remember much about my father. He was knighted for bravery during the Crimean War, after which he deserted my mother and me to dig for gold in Australia. We heard he struck it rich and bought land in America. There was no more news until his solicitors wrote to inform me that I had inherited seventy thousand acres in someplace called Idaho Territory. When I got here I learned that I owed more than the ranch was worth. I could have walked away. Instead I wrote Sheffield, where my father still had friends, and offered them controlling interest in return for payment of debts and the post of manager. They accepted, and since then I've done nothing but regret my action."

While he was speaking, Jim Stemmer came through the batwing doors and demanded whiskey at the bar, ignoring the chorus of jeers that greeted him. It struck Fulwider that he smelled much worse than North had the day he and his brother forced his hand. He drank up, paid and left, raking a murderous glance over both Meredith and the journalist that made Fulwider wonder if he remembered him from Bismarck. The doors flapped to behind him.

The Englishman was saying something about Dale Crippen. He concentrated on the words.

". . . not for him I would never have survived those first few weeks. He knew far more about cattle and horses than any four men I've met out here. He is sorely missed."

Fulwider sorted through his journalist's vocabulary for

adequate phrases of consolation. He could find none. He sipped his cognac and found that it tasted as much like stewed barbed wire as always.

"You've changed," Meredith observed. He'd placed his hat on the table, revealing again the lines of age under his ice-blue eyes and at the corners of his aristocratic nostrils.

"The doctor assures me I'll start putting on weight soon," said the other, drawing patterns with his forefinger among the beads of moisture on the outside of his glass.

"That's not what I meant. I mean that you have grown hard. You're not the gullible easterner I met two months ago."

"I'd like to believe that, but a week in the wilderness doesn't make a Kit Carson out of a Horace Greeley."

"Perhaps not, ordinarily. But your experiences during that week were hardly ordinary. A lesser man would have succumbed."

"A wiser one would not have gone in the first place. But you didn't ask me in here to discuss either my wisdom or my fortitude."

He laughed quietly and dampened his lips once again. It had taken him almost twenty minutes to drain the glass the first time. "Would you call Asa North your friend?"

"No man calls him that."

"You saved his life. You must have developed some sort of rapport."

"Why?"

Meredith leaned forward onto his forearms. "I want you to get in touch with him. He's the only man capable of running Black Jack to ground before my investment in this territory is literally eaten up."

Fulwider drank. "Wolves don't plague cattle in the springtime. There is too much risk in it when other prey is available."

"I wish you'd explain that to my fellow investors."

"Do they trouble you?"

"Like Penelope's suitors." He smiled at his own witticism. "Hardly a month passes without a letter from one or another, asking where are all the profits von Richthofen promised in his book about ranching on the plains. Those I can handle, though I suspect at least one of them is entertaining dangerous notions about my integrity. But Black Jack is another matter."

"They know about him?"

"You aren't the first writer to sense a story here. A year ago, a fellow in Boston somehow acquired a number of clippings about the animal from the Boise newspaper and put together a lurid account that sold for a dime on the east coast. Someone sent a copy to someone else in England. Rumors began circulating—outlandish tales, the kind one might expect from a country where wolves have been extinct for four hundred years. Now my associates are demanding that I do something about the problem or sacrifice my position."

"Wouldn't that solve your problem?" Fulwider posed.

"I won't leave here in disgrace!" The rancher slammed his fist to the table, spilling their drinks and stopping all conversation in the room. Embarrassed, he sat back and lowered his voice. "I won't give my friends here that satisfaction. When I leave, it will be by my decision. That's why I need North."

"There are other wolfers."

He shook his head. "When you are dealing with a myth you must use mythical means to combat it. The only way I can reassure those people is to employ a legend to pursue a legend. We are speaking of intangibles here, not just of a man and a wolf."

"I haven't the slightest idea where to begin looking for

him. And even if I found him I can't say I could persuade him to return. He is a deeply troubled man."

"He isn't the only one who has lost something out here," came the bitter reply.

"If you mean Dale Crippen, they were far from friends."

"Not that. The other thing."

Something in the journalist's expression must have betrayed his bewilderment, for the rancher stared at him in disbelief. "You didn't know?"

"Know what?"

"It's part of the legend." He drew himself upright and stared into the amber liquid in his glass as if the details of his narrative were to be found there. The story he told had the symmetry of something shaped by repetition around countless campfires.

Asa North had taken a Cheyenne woman in marriage and gone to live with her in Montana's Bighorn Mountains. Because her name was unpronounceable in her native tongue he called her Leah, though no one was clear why he chose that name in particular. There was a child, a dark-eyed girl in whom the combination of her father's tawny hair and her mother's dusky features was as attractive as it was striking, and whose childish curiosity and determination to satisfy it no matter what the consequences won her the nickname of Cat.

Cat was two years old the winter her father returned from trading with the Arapaho to find his cabin dark and the chimney cold. The snow was deep, and though he had started back in the forenoon it was dusk by the time he made the discovery. He nearly killed his horse plunging through the drifts that stood between him and the door.

Inside, the cabin was black and silent. He fumbled for a lantern and matches and waited impatiently as the wick's reddish glow spread outward, fading and yellowing. Monstrous shadows slithered up the walls as he turned the tiny key.

He saw the girl first, and gagged on his own vomit.

She was lying in the cradle he had made for her—placed there, probably, by her mother after the convulsions had begun. Her own seizures would then have driven Leah to their pallet, where he found her wrapped in the colorful blanket presented them by her uncle, a powerful sub-chief, on the occasion of their wedding. In earthen dishes on the table he discovered fresh venison remains, and from them he learned what had happened.

Not understanding poison, she would have diagnosed the cramps that seized her and her child as another of the strange diseases the white man brought from the East, and would have been powerless to deal with them. When she had found the deer lying near the cabin it wouldn't have occurred to her to question the boon, or suspect that it had lapped at the snow where a wolf had vomited the strychnine that was killing it or where a careless wolfer had dropped a crystal while tainting a carcass. Deer, like children, are curious, and like children they are apt to put anything in their mouths that interests them. Being unaware of the campaign of extinction going on among the Montana wolf population, she would have no reason to avoid the meat. She had watched her child die and then had succumbed herself without ever knowing why.

In the end it was not their deaths that haunted him so much as the image of their faces and what the poison had done to them in the final throes, so that the memories he kept of the good times were obscured forever behind those hideous, scarcely human grins. They returned to him in nightmares even now, and he woke up screaming Leah's name.

Fulwider didn't say anything for a long time after Meredith had finished. At the bar, glasses clinked and liquor gurgled hollowly from vessel to vessel. He swallowed the last of his brandy and stood up.

"I can't help you," he said. "I have no way of reaching North. Perhaps the Stemmers can find Black Jack, assuming Aaron still has a taste for wolf."

The rancher looked sour. "Aaron doesn't know a wolf from a jackass. Turning his brother and him loose on New-castle would be like giving them a license to rustle."

There was nothing Fulwider could say to comfort him. He thanked him for the drinks and left. On his way out he heard Meredith ordering another refill.

In the lobby of the Assiniboin he was approached by a boy in overalls carrying an envelope, who asked him if he was R. G. Fulwider. The journalist tipped him and opened a telegram signed by the editor, informing him that his first-hand account of the wolfing trip in the Caribous would run the last week of April and congratulating him upon a fine job. He crumpled it and tossed it into the wastebasket be-hind the clerk's desk.

He paused before the door of his room, dreading the same four walls he had been staring at for weeks. After a full minute he turned and descended the steps back to the ground floor. Thanatopsis blinked as he passed the desk but made no comment.

The unmarked building across from the hotel sported a fresh coat of paint and a bell pull. Fulwider's jangle was answered by a short, buxom woman with copper-dyed hair and eyes that protruded under lids tinted a disconcerting shade of green. Before he could stammer out his business, she ushered him inside with a sweeping gesture of her thick and not entirely feminine right arm.

"I have been expecting you since first you came to town," said she, in a surprisingly deep voice coarsened by a heavy German accent. "I am Aurora. Ladies, there is a gentleman here I would like you to meet."

The large front parlor was elegant if overdecorated, with narrow aisles winding among pedestal tables and skirt-legged chairs and sofas piled with lacy cushions and a gramophone on a low stand, playing a scratchy, nasal rendition of "Whispering Hope." Heavy curtains drawn over the windows made necessary a number of burning lamps, whose oily smell mingled with the scent of too many varieties of toilet water in a closed space to sour the liquor in his stomach. The various seats were occupied by women in flowered kimonos who studied him with lidded eyes.

He selected the youngest of the group, a blonde of about thirty, paid in advance and escorted her up the stairs to the second story. When he came down Asa North was waiting for him inside the front door.

# TWELVE

He looked tired. His tall moccasins were mud-heavy and his clothes, including the matted and tangled wolfskin, were coated with a fine yellow dust that sifted from him when he moved. Even his face was caked, lending him a jaundiced appearance. In his presence, Fulwider forgot the evil mixture of scent and coal oil that had assailed him upon entering the overdone parlor, and smelled again those odors of wolf and leather and sweat of horse and man with which he had come to associate North alone. The yellow-brown eyes fixed on him when he came to the landing and didn't waver as the journalist hastened down to greet him with hand outstretched.

"Hope I didn't interrupt nothing." His palm was like an asbestos glove.

"How long have you been in town?" Fulwider spoke quickly to cover his embarrassment. His blonde companion had somehow melted away at the head of the stairs. Indeed, the parlor itself was deserted but for them. The wolfer had that effect on people, like some fearsome wild thing that wandered occasionally from its natural habitat, to be let alone until it left.

"An hour, I reckon. Long enough to talk to Meredith."

"He found you?"

"I found him. He offered to up the bounty to two thousand."

"Did you accept?"

He stirred restlessly in the closeness of the room. Fulwider understood and accompanied him out onto the porch. The sky looked like rain. There were lights in some of the other buildings and a cool, wet breeze carried laughter and cigar smoke from the Timber Queen next door.

"I said I'd do it for the twelve hunnert we agreed on." The broad brim of North's hat cast his profile into somber relief against the lighted window of the general merchandise. He seemed most alone when he was in the midst of people. "I was in Rock Springs buying cartridges when it come to me I let a wolf get the better of me. I backtracked near three hundred miles for another shot at it."

"I assumed you had business elsewhere."

"My business is wolfing."

The conversation faltered at that point, and for a time they watched and listened as the occasional rider trotted down the street and tied up in front of the saloon. They stepped off the porch to allow a trio of dusty cowboys entrance to the house of ill fame. Inside, someone rewound the gramophone and "Whispering Hope" drifted out on the damp air.

"They get that half-breed Lightfoot?" North asked then.

Fulwider shook his head. "The sheriff got up a posse and combed the Caribou foothills. They found where he'd come back to bury Sam Fire Eye, but that was all. His description has been wired to every community within two hundred miles. It's only a matter of time before he's arrested or shot."

"Maybe."

High in the mountains, a jagged streak of lightning shattered the shadows and withdrew. Moments later thunder rumbled in the distance.

"Got anything keeping you here?"

Fulwider paused, absorbing his meaning. He watched North closely. "Why do you ask?"

"Some wolves call for two men."

"You can't mean me. There are other wolfers. Real wolfers."

"I don't much get on with other wolfers. They talk too much. So do you, but you don't get mad when I don't pay mind."

"That's no reason."

"It's as close to one as you'll get."

It struck the journalist suddenly that he was being paid a great compliment. He felt himself flushing with schoolboy pride. "I'm decaying here," he said, with as much nonchalance as he could muster. "I will go with you."

"Something you should know. I invited two others. You may know them, Jim and Aaron Stemmer."

He stared. "Why, in the name of heaven?"

"Little idea of my own. They ain't much at wolfing, but word is they can shuck skin like a snake. With them along we can set up a relay. All you and I got to do is shoot wolves and keep moving. They'll follow with a pack string, yank the skins and send back for the bounty. One follows and skins, the other goes back for the money and comes back for more pelts. That way we can stay out as long as it takes to run down Black Jack. Just like a buffalo hunt."

It was the longest speech the journalist had ever heard him deliver. "Have you talked to them about it?"

"After I saw Meredith," he nodded. "Aaron was ready to do anything to keep from eating the rest of that wolf. They'll be getting a fifty-fifty split on the regular bounties. The big one's yours and mine."

"How do you know they won't just collect the bounty and leave? Especially after what you did to Aaron last month in Bismark."

"They thought about it. I seen it in their eyes. They won't."

"But how do you know?"

"Because I told them they wouldn't."

He spoke matter-of-factly in that quiet tone that reminded Fulwider of an animal's warning growl. Jim Stemmer might not have understood it, but the journalist pictured his brother fingering the scar on his abdomen and knew that North was right.

"Did you tell them about Black Jack?"

"They asked about him. I said he's not their never-mind. They won't be helping us get him."

"You don't really care about the bounty, do you? All you want is the wolf. He's the reason you came back all this way."

"He's a wolf like any other." He started walking. Fulwider caught up with him and they started across to the hotel.

"When do we leave?" he asked, though he knew the answer.

"First light."

Assigned to select a pack animal for the journey—a task which in itself attested to the wolfer's confidence in his judgment—Fulwider was astonished to find the stout black he had left behind at the river calmly munching oats in the livery stable. In the barber shop next door he interviewed the German owner of both establishments, who informed him in broken English and with much gesturing that the posse had found the horse during its search for Dale Crippen's killer and that for the price of the animal's care he was free to take it away. He paid the amount gladly, explaining that he would come for it the next morning.

Sheriff Adamson, the omnipresent shotgun dangling at his side, was waiting for him when he came out. He had overheard the conversation.

"Planning a trip?"

Briefly, Fulwider described the mission. The Swede listened in silence, a solid fat man who tapered upward and downward from a huge middle, but whose small, bright eyes spared him the appearance of plodding dullness the journalist had observed in many men of great girth.

"I am relieved," he said then. "I was afraid that perhaps you were planning to avenge your friend's death by finding and killing Dick Lightfoot."

"I assure you, the thought never crossed our minds."

Adamson shrugged. "It is sheriff's suspicion. No man is who he claims he is and nothing he says is to be believed." But he didn't sound apologetic.

"We are hunting for wolves," stressed the other, "not men."

"Yes, you said that."

"I don't think you believed me either time."

He sighed heavily. "Before North came, there was only one murder here since my election, when old Mrs. Pollard was strangled with a leather halter for the jar of gold coins she kept buried in her pantry. I am still looking for her killer. The jail will hold only two prisoners at a time, and when I catch him and Dick Lightfoot I will need the space."

"What are you trying to say, Sheriff?"

"Only that I know this man North. I know what he did to Aaron Stemmer in Bismarck. A man like that will kill without having to think twice. I would hate to see him drag you down with him."

Fulwider said nothing. The fat man nodded as if he had.

"Just see that you kill wolves only." He moved off down the street, swaying from side to side with elephantine grace.

The journalist returned to the hotel deep in thought.

# THIRTEEN

The Stemmers proved disagreeable companions from the start.

Fulwider's first premonition came when Aaron, evil-eyed and still belching from his bizarre meal of the previous morning, wasted a half-hour of daylight searching for his brother, whom he had left swilling whiskey in the Timber Queen at 1 A.M. He was discovered at last dozing in the woodbox behind Aurora's place, after which another twenty minutes was lost sobering him up with the aid of a horse trough full of icy water. By that time the weather the journalist had seen yesterday in the mountains had reached town, and the expedition moved out through hissing rain.

When Jim and Aaron weren't arguing between themselves, they complained about the weather, the condition of the trail, the plodding pace and the disposition of the pack string, two short-coupled chestnuts and a bay gelding with an ill temper and a wandering eye. These carried the brothers' supplies and would be used to transport the skins. North's white-stockinged black bore his and Fulwider's provisions at the end of a halter attached to its master's saddle. It didn't get along with the others, hence the separation. Up front, Fulwider rode his gray, North the wily roan.

In general, Aaron appeared to have forgotten his injury at the wolfer's hands, or at least to have pushed it aside in view of the profits to be gained from the partnership. He had the largest vocabulary of curses the journalist had ever heard. His chief dislikes, in order of their importance, were Republicans, Socialists, Catholics (he was a Lutheran), President Cleveland, Nelson Meredith and the Territory of Idaho, the Snake River Valley in particular. He was vocal about all of them, and seemed oblivious to the fact that no one cared what he had to say about any of them.

Jim, on the other hand, was inclined to smolder in sullen silence, eyes on the road ahead and his blond moustache damp and drooping under the shapeless brim of his hat. Fulwider wondered if this was an effect of his dissipation or an indication of his true nature. If it was the latter he would bear close scrutiny.

The scenery was almost unrecognizable since the thaw. Gone was winter's barren whitewash, exposing green hills sprinkled with wildflowers in red and yellow and violet. In the foreground, budding branches of birch and oak and maple reached for the rain-sodden sky, while in the distance the worn sawtooth line of the Caribous stood out like something not of nature, cut out hastily and pasted on the horizon, playing hell with perspective for their seeming closeness. The riders' breath showed in quick gray jets against the icy downfall and steam rose from the horses' withers.

They encountered no wolf signs the first day, nor did they seek them. Rain beat the road into brown soup and obliterated their own tracks almost as they were made. Even the river had changed, and was now a howling torrent sixty feet wide clawing at the banks and girdling trees that shook and shed bark and buds into the current. Finding that the ford no longer existed, the four crossed a mile farther down at sunset and camped on a rise overlooking the south bank. For lack of dry firewood they made a cold camp, using their oilcloth slickers for tents and eating sardines with their fingers from the cans. Afterward they curled up for a miserably cold night while drops pattered the makeshift shelters. Fulwider took a bottle with him to stifle his cough.

They were up and moving again before dawn. The rain had stopped, but as the sky turned pale a lead-colored mist crept into the hollows, making the trees that spiked up from it look as if they were floating two feet above the ground. The overcast remained.

Two hours later, the sun wedged itself through a crack in the clouds, forcing them apart and lifting the fog in a body, so that as the riders moved through it the vapor parted and drifted skyward like smoke rings in a room with a high ceiling. Drying, their clothes shed steam like damp overcoats hung next to a stove. By noon all but North had stripped off their jackets.

They encountered their first wolf droppings toward dusk of the second day, near a bramble at the base of the canyon wall. But these were weeks old, and North scarcely acknowledged them. They began climbing. A third of the way up the incline, the wolfer exclaimed softly and drew rein, leaping to the ground in the same movement.

He squatted over an indentation in a moist patch of bare earth surrounded by saber-like blades of grass. The track was as large as a man's hand and the claw marks were clearly visible even from horseback.

"Last night or early this morning," he declared. "Since the rain."

"A loner?" suggested Fulwider. There were no other prints in sight.

"Not likely. He's too young and too healthy to be cast out."

Irritation swept through the the journalist, prodded by his discomfort. "That's the second time you've said something like that. How can you tell just from the track?"

North rose, his skins rustling. "This one was running. Toes deep, rear pad shallow. Old ones don't go in much for speed. Sick ones, hydrophobic and like that, tense up so that the toes are all bunched together. You learn to look for that after a spell."

"He's right," said Aaron, who then began a narrative about a wolf he had tracked in Wyoming. Fulwider interrupted him.

"I'll remember that." North had shamed him with his patient explanation.

"Don't bother." The wolfer mounted. "It won't do you any good."

Camp that evening was a different prospect. The food was hot, and even Jim Stemmer showed signs of coming out of his funk. He set aside his clean plate and produced a jew's-harp, plucking out a sprightly tune while his brother told of a wolfer they had both known in Colorado.

"He was a full-blooded Ute," he began, spitting out a piece of unraveled cigar and touching off the end with a stick from the fire. "His right name was Son-of-a Bitch or something like that—"

"Sun-in-the-Eyes," Jim corrected, and resumed playing.

"Yeah, something like that. But most folks called him Crooked Mouth Hank on account of he had this scar on his lip that made one side of it look higher than the other. Anyway, he could find a wolf that had died of old age and track it back to where it was born. I went hunting with him one time and figured it out. When a white man goes out tracking, he's thinking about his wife or his whore or what he's eaten for breakfast that morning or if he's going to stop off for a quick one before heading home—a thousand things that don't got nothing to do with why he's out there. A injun, he's thinking about one thing only, and that's what he's tracking. He can't handle but one thing at a time, just like a animal. That's why he's so good at everything he does.''

The dregs from North's cup made an angry hissing noise when he cast them into the flames. ''Get to sleep,'' he said, rising.

Fulwider heard the Stemmers snickering between themselves as they unlimbered their bedrolls. They knew the story of North's Cheyenne wife and daughter, and the effect of Aaron's crude comment about Indians had been calculated. So he hadn't forgotten old animosities after all.

Hours later the journalist awoke with his throat closed tight and a screaming need for air. It was still pitch black. He sat up gasping and fumbled the bottle out of his saddle pouch. As he tipped it up there was a crash in the bushes fifty yards away and a sound of feet retreating rapidly. He listened, his mouth full of liquor. After half a minute he swallowed slowly, letting the warming fluid trickle down and widen the opening. When he could breathe normally he packed away the vessel, but before settling back down he picked up his Remington and tucked it beside him under the blanket. Whether he actually heard them or not, those footsteps had sounded human.

The days were noticeably longer than on the first expedition, and unencumbered by snow and ice the party made far better time. The following afternoon found them on the high plain where the earlier trip had come to its shattering conclusion. As they neared the desolate scene, Fulwider's heart grew sick at the sight of the bones of elk and wolf, picked clean by scavengers and all but hidden by the tall

new grass. The change of seasons had relegated them to
the dead past, Dale Crippen included. It was hard to believe
that only a few weeks had come and gone since the close
of the drama.

Aaron Stemmer made a discovery and hailed them over.
Upon the spot where the half-breed wolfer had lain riddled
with bullets was a mound of fresh earth. A flat shard of
birchwood had been jammed roughly into the earth at one
end, a crude legend carved across its smooth white surface.

> **sam fire eye Under This bord**
> **is sum uv his bones**
> **all the varmints left cudnt**
> **find the skul Murdered**

"That's real pretty, like a poem," Aaron commented.
"Jim, something was to happen to me I'd take it right kind
if you would stick up a marker like that over me. Other
way around, I'd do you the same."

Jim, who up to that point appeared to have fallen back
into his earlier unresponsive mood, replied dryly that if it
was all the same to his brother he'd just as soon be eaten
by coyotes and ravens.

"We should of took time to scratch up that grave," said
North, as they approached the base of the high peaks. They
were his first words since before they had come upon the
makeshift headboard.

"What would you expect to find, other than a few
bones?" Fulwider asked.

He didn't answer for another hundred yards. Then:

"I done some asking in town. Sam Fire Eye's mother
was Cheyenne but he was raised up white in his father's
house. He took the injun name after he left. Dick Lightfoot

was the other way around—Cheyenne pa, brung up sav-age.''

''So?''

''So who give Sam a Christian burial?''

# FOURTEEN

Fulwider was still pondering his partner's words when North stopped suddenly. The journalist reined in an instant later, not in time to catch more than a fleeting glimpse of a gray form darting over a rise some three hundred yards west. The others jingled to a halt behind, but by that time the leaders were moving again, cantering in the direction of the sun's descent. When they reached the rise they could see nothing beyond the next.

"Figured," said North, leaning on his pommel. "Bitch."

"How can you tell?"

He pointed out a flat rock roughly the size of a human torso, perched at a slight angle with one end buried in the soil before his roan's forefeet. The surface was littered with gray hairs, many in tufts. Fulwider's gray caught the predator's scent and fought the bit.

"That's where she was bedded. They start shedding around the belly during denning season. Makes it easier for the whelps to get at the milk. I seen she was pink underneath when she spooked."

"From that distance? All I saw was a blur."

"That's because you wasn't thinking wolf."

"And you were?"

"All the time. Just like an injun."

There was no sarcasm in his tone, and from the look on the Stemmers' faces it was hard to tell if they had picked up on the offhand reference to Aaron's conversation of last night.

"There she is!" Aaron lifted his Winchester, which like North he was in the habit of carrying across his saddle. At the top of the next ridge stood the she-wolf, broadside with her head turned in their direction. Outlined as she was against the sky, her mammaries were clearly visible and clearly hairless.

"I kilt more curious wolves than any other kind," Aaron gloated, taking careful aim.

North stretched a long arm clear across the neck of Fulwider's horse and wrenched the carbine from Stemmer's grasp with a sudden exertion. Startled, he pulled at the Colt in his belt. Fulwider looped his reins around the barrel just as it came up and yanked, flipping it out of Aaron's hand. By that time the wolfer had both brothers covered with his Ballard.

"If you can't hang onto a gun, don't carry one," he said.

The journalist was in a mild state of shock, partly from the violence that had almost come to pass and partly because of his role in averting it. He had acted from reflex, and even now wasn't sure exactly what he had done.

The look in Aaron's eye was murderous. "Now you went and scared her off. What is she, a pet?" He spat the words.

"Her den's close by," North explained. "She ain't about to stray far after just whelping." He returned the Winchester.

"So her den's close by." The other fingered the carbine and glowered. "So what?"

"So have you ever heard of a mother wolf bringing up her pups alone?"

Fulwider took charge of the wolfer's rifle and reins while he dismounted. When he was halfway up the next slope he sank into a crouch and finally onto all fours, crawling the rest of the way to the top. Even in that awkward posture he moved with the grace of a splendid animal, as if he found it more natural than walking erect. The journalist worried lest one of the others in his excitement mistake the nearly supine figure in the gray fur for a wolf and shoot him on the spot.

After some minutes of motionless observance from the crest, however, North reversed himself and straightened to trot back in their direction. He helped himself to a draft from his canteen.

"She's alone," he said, wiping his mouth on the back of his hand and replacing the cap. "Just her and the den. Whelps wouldn't be old enough to come out into the open yet. Reckon she come here for a rest from all that sucking and squealing."

"Got to be a male someplace," Aaron observed. He had retrieved his Colt from the ground and was blowing dirt and bits of grass from the action.

"There usually is, or she wouldn't have young ones." The irony in this statement wasn't evident in North's tone. "More than one, by the signs. The others will be out hunting. If we stick it out till dusk we might could have us a proper stand."

There were no objections, least of all from Fulwider, who had no idea what was meant by the term "stand." The four led their animals into the depression ahead and left them to graze while they crawled on hands and knees to the top under the wolfer's direction, flattening out on their stomachs in the tall grass.

Slabs of shale that had tumbled from the mountains eons past lay in piles at the base, between which clumps of brush and stately lodgepole pines forced their way into the sunlight. From there the ground rose first in a steady grade, then ever steeper until it pierced the clouds. The sun glared off the ice a thousand feet up and coaxed a million tiny sparkles out of the bare granite beneath.

The journalist saw nothing that resembled either a wolf or what he thought a den should look like, until North joined him and pointed out a triangular opening less than eighteen inches across in a rockfall thirty yards dead ahead. It hardly looked like something a full-grown wolf would choose to drag itself through. Yet the other assured him that he had seen the mother slink into its depths only minutes before.

"She's had her rest," North murmured. "She won't be coming out again before the others show up."

The pack, he explained, would approach from the brush that girded the mountain. "One thing." He spoke so quietly Fulwider had to cock his head to hear. "Black Jack's mine. If there's more than one bullet in him when he falls and they ain't both mine, it'll be just too bad for someone."

No elaboration was needed. The easterner passed the ominous message to Aaron, who lay on the other side of him. Protest flickered in his close-set brown eyes, then faded. He whispered to his brother. Jim's only reaction was to push out his moustache and tug down the dilapidated brim of his hat. Neither appeared to doubt the wolfer's ability to back up his threat. The four made themselves as comfortable as possible for the long wait.

Fulwider dozed, or thought he had. He opened his eyes after what seemed only a moment to see that everything was bathed in gray wash. The sun's last rays described a bloody gash over the range's western sweep. Almost immediately the journalist noted a tension in the air, like the oppressive stillness that precedes a sudden cloudburst. The men beside him were stiff as rods. Even the wind had ceased for the moment. It was as if the whole world were holding its breath.

They came trickling down the eastern face like drops down a glass, without pattern and seemingly leaderless as they negotiated the descent through a sparse stand of lodgepole pine near the base. In the eerie twilight the gray shapes slunk in and out of view among trees and shadow, now visible, now not, now materializing a hundred feet lower, six ghosts gliding over stone and sparse grass and springs that glistened like quicksilver under the rising moon. They made no more noise than peals of fog, which in their effortless movement they resembled.

As they neared the bottom, the scattered shapes drew into an amorphous, moving mass from which a narrow tongue slithered presently, revealing itself in a shaft of dying sunlight as a line of animals advancing in single file. At that point the men watching were presented with their first clear view of the newcomers, one the journalist would never forget.

The wolf in front was a big male, steel gray, with a well-developed ruff and a black mantle that covered his head cowl-fashion and extended back over his shoulders. There it narrowed into a thin edge along the spine before disappearing into a brush tail, held horizontally in an attitude suggesting dominance. White hairs in his muzzle bespoke age, but his heavy frame would have discouraged many of the younger males from testing his leadership. There were some, however, who had not discouraged so easily, as demonstrated by the various slash-like scars on his face and shoulders. It was an expressive face, with almond-shaped eyes that tilted down from a square muzzle, and a wide mouth drawn taut as in concentration. A leader's face clearly, strong and worried.

Directly behind him crept a smaller wolf whose coat was as white as any ermine Fulwider had seen adorning a fine lady's shoulders in Manhattan. This would be Black Jack's mate, and a worthy queen she appeared, with her dark eyes and black nose and coal lips that stood out strikingly from their snowy background. He had never beheld a creature more beautiful.

In winter the beasts' coats were a wonderful combination of heavy, butter-soft fur overlain with waterproof guard hairs growing as long as five inches at their throats and shoulders, where the ruff was so thick no claw or fang could penetrate to the vulnerable flesh beneath. The shedding season was well along, but even now the coarse outer layer remained largely intact. Thus, while the creatures might have appeared to decrease in bulk during warm weather, they didn't look as if they'd been on the losing end of a fight with a wildcat, as had the buffalo once their coats began to fall away in bloody patches.

A startling change overtook the pack as they neared the den. The mother whom they had left behind to care for her pups emerged to greet them with a joyous little yip, where upon they abandoned caution and became nothing more sinister than a family of big, friendly dogs. Their sides were full from the day's hunt, and as they loped panting toward the waiting female their tongues lolled out of their mouths and they barked and whimpered like pets at play.

And play they did. Before Fulwider's amazed eyes, these scourges of the northwestern cattle industry, hated and hunted from the Bering coast to the Gulf of Mexico, leaped and tumbled and butted each other and touched noses and carried on generally as if blood and bounties were things that had nothing to do with them. The noise was like that in a kennel, only gayer, more carefree. For North had chosen his stand well: The wind was blowing in the wrong direction for the quarry to know they were being watched.

And then they knew, but by then it was too late.

## FIFTEEN

Aaron's Winchester spoke first, followed closely by his brother's rifle, a muzzle-loader whose *ka-pow* sounded like a stuttering echo to the cleaner report of the carbine.

There was confusion in the vicinity of the den. Wolves fell, but there was so much frantic movement around them that it was impossible to tell which had been hit. North's Ballard barked at a stately pace, letting the Stemmers' weapons release four bullets to its one. Blue smoke coarse as wire drifted back from the flaming muzzles and enveloped the shooters' heads, trapped under their hat brims. After each shot, Jim produced a powder horn, caps and a sack of lead balls, loaded the antique piece, tamped down the wadding and fired again almost as fast as his brother could lever a fresh round into the chamber of the repeater.

The animals near the den had scattered. One, whose black mantle Fulwider could barely make out in the gathering darkness, yelped loudly and went down, but was up again in an instant and bounding on three legs for the cover farther up. North reloaded, his fingers moving swiftly but surely as he replaced the spent cartridge from the leather pouch he carried on his belt. But his target was faster by

half a beat, and as he made ready to fire again the creature's
brush tail vanished into the foliage. The wolfer sent a bullet
after him. A swiftly moving mass slid noisily through the
scrub, followed by silence.

"Some shot," Aaron sneered, in the stillness that followed on the heels of the last report. His face was black
with spent powder. "I could of dropped him if you let me."

"If I wanted you to, I would of." There was no trace of
disappointment in the wolfer's speech. Again he reloaded.
"I didn't hear that Remington."

"No," replied Fulwider, "you didn't."

North glanced at him, but by then their features were
invisible.

It was dark, as if Black Jack had dragged the last shred
of daylight with him into the bushes. The air stank harshly
of rotten eggs from the sulphur in the powder. North stirred,
rose, and was heard walking away in the direction of the
horses. Miscellaneous noises sounded, a match flared presently, followed a moment later by a spreading glow as a
lantern was ignited. Its yellow illumination erased the
weathered creases in the wolfer's face; for the first time
since they had met, the journalist was struck by Asa North's
youth. Coming back up the hill he looked no older than
some of the copy boys at the *World*. This reminded Fulwider of the scarcity of truly old people in the West, and
suddenly he felt quite ancient at forty.

As North drew near carrying the lantern, its light fell
across the others standing with Fulwider in a semicircle
where they had been lying in ambush. Spaced in this fashion they had effectively sealed off every line of retreat for
their prey save one, the mountain itself. There was something eerily familiar about the arrangement that eluded the
easterner until he remembered that Black Jack's party had
employed the same tactic in bringing down the straggling

elk a few weeks before. He strongly doubted that it was a coincidence.

Four wolves lay in the clearing, a fifth in the rocky perimeter of the den. North raised the lantern over the others. The glow fell across the body of the white female. A glistening dark streak marred its pale side where an ounce of lead had torn a furrow before entering the heart behind the left foreleg. Her eyes shone softly in the coal oil light.

Three were male, one smaller than the others and evidently a yearling. The largest of the trio lay at the extreme edge of the clearing, where it had been shot a second time while limping for cover. The first had smashed one of its hind paws, but the other had struck it behind the ear and carried away most of its head on the way out. That would have been a ball from Jim's big muzzle-loader.

North stepped over to the den, where the mother wolf lay panting.

Blood seeped through a hole in her chest and bubbled obscenely in her mouth and nostrils as her breath passed in and out with a sucking sound. Her amber eyes watched North as if to determine whether he was an ally or an enemy. They were intelligent eyes, almost human. A tiny reflection of the lantern flickered in each pupil. Then there was a deafening crash, her entire body heaved as though trying to rise, fell back with a grunt of escaping air and lay twitching. The left side of her head was gone. Soon the twitching stopped. Smoke found its way out of the barrel of the Ballard.

A quiet moment followed. Then came a sound that wrenched Fulwider's heart from its moorings. Something was squeaking far back in the den.

"The pups," he whispered.

"Clean forgot about them." North paused, the pale light playing off the angular bones of his face. "Who does it?"

"Me," said Aaron. "Providing Jim and me get the bounty." His brother nodded support.

The wolfer looked doubtful. "Think you'll fit?"

Jim said, "Don't let the way he's built fool you. He's mostly muscle."

"Yeah, I seen it hanging over his belt. Get to it, then."

Stemmer relieved himself of hat, coat and weapons, and with Jim's help lifted the limp carcass of the mother away from the entrance by its legs. It left a dark patch behind. Then he sank onto his hands and knees and crawled through the narrow opening, grunting as he squeezed between the boulders. His bulk muffled the whining sounds issuing from below ground.

For several minutes he struggled, dragging himself forward an inch at a time on his stomach, until only the thick soles of his boots were still exposed. The noises grew more frantic as he advanced. They didn't sound frightened. To Fulwider they were the joyous yip-yaps common to pups everywhere when greeting what they thought was their mother. At that age they wouldn't understand fear.

For a moment Aaron was motionless. Then his bootsoles twitched as if seeking leverage. One by one the noises rose to shrieks and ceased.

He kicked his right foot twice in the manner of a signal. Immediately Jim stepped forward and, grasping one of his brother's ankles in each hand, pulled him backward out of the hole. Moments later Aaron, disheveled, sweating, streaked with dirt, got up displaying his trophies: Four small, round, furry objects, two in each hand, their little necks squeezed between thumbs and forefingers. Quite dead.

"That all there was in the litter?" North asked.

Stemmer shrugged. "Association's offering two bucks apiece for whelps. Money's money."

Fulwider was aware that Jim was staring at him. "What's your problem, tenderfoot?" he said. "You don't look so good."

He didn't reply. Instead he stepped away into the shadows and was sick as quietly as he could manage.

"Suit yourself."

In the moist light of dawn, Asa North studied a patch of blood the size of a dinner-plate staining the sparse grass a hundred feet up the mountainside. He had finished his breakfast, as had the Stemmers, who were busy skinning the dead wolves below. Fulwider, not quite ready to trust his stomach, had refused everything but coffee.

"Aren't you curious about why I'm leaving?" the journalist demanded, irritated by the wolfer's brusqueness.

"I know why. You found out we strangle whelps and now you don't like us no more."

"It isn't that. It's just that I've lost my enthusiasm for the hunt."

North turned on him, cold malevolence in his stare.

"What the hell did you expect? We was going to take their pictures? I told you before you wasn't cut out to be no kind of wolfer."

"Then why did you ask me along this time? I'm still not clear on that."

"Why did you say yes?"

Fulwider made no response, and the wolfer resumed his scrutiny of the rusty patch.

A warm wind was gusting up from the flatlands, one of those southerly chinooks that hastened the thaw and made summers unbearably hot away from the high country. It felt good, though it did little to dispel a chill in the journalist's bones not entirely due to the night he'd spent on the damp, marshy ground that flanked the mountains.

Sometime during that long night, as he lay staring up at the charcoal-wash of the sky, his interest in the fate of Black Jack and of the men who hunted him had evaporated. The speech he had made to North about going back had run through his head ten thousand times before it found its way past his tongue. But he could see that it was lost on the wolfer.

"He's wasted a heap of blood." As usual the comment seemed directed more to North himself than to the journalist. "He'll be looking for cover till it stops."

"Well, good-bye." Fulwider held out an awkward hand, made more so by the other's refusal to acknowledge it. As he turned to leave:

"Cut out your share of the provisions and hold to that elk run on your way back. That way you won't be so likely to get lost."

Fulwider thanked him and walked away.

"The guy was from Minnesota, fancied himself a wolfer."

Aaron Stemmer's foghorn voice was raised to carry to the man transferring supplies from the black to his own saddle pouches. Arms bare and bloodied to the elbows, the brothers labored cheerfully over the slain wolves.

"Said he didn't hold with strangling wolves. So he taken this here English forty-five he set some store by and crawled down into the den and started blasting away right and left like it was the goddamn Fourth of July. Clean busted both his eardrums."

Fulwider hoisted himself up and over the gray while their laughter welled over him.

The sun burned off the morning mist early and lay like a warm shawl on his shoulders. After an hour he shrugged out of his jacket, stowing it behind his cantle. By mid-morning, however, he had reached the ledge overlooking the river, and the cool, damp air wafting up from its banks forced him to put it back on. Later he would remember that as the decision that saved his life.

A mile farther on he came to a stop where a rockfall blocked his path. Twenty feet above, blue daylight showed through a notch where the wall had collapsed scant hours before. He dismounted to lead the reluctant horse over the mound of jagged granite.

Something struck his left shoulder. He lost his footing and staggered back several steps, swinging his arms to regain his balance on the very edge of the precipice. Beneath his heels he glimpsed the fuzzy tops of the two hundred-foot pines that skirted the river. He stepped away, heart pounding.

His shoulder felt stiff. Deciding that a rock had bounded off it from the top of the broken wall, he bent to pick up his reins and gasped as a sharp, stinging pain coursed through him. He reached back to feel his shoulder.

His fingers closed around the hilt of a knife buried in the flesh. Then his legs gave away and he pitched backward into space.

## SIXTEEN

As in some hideous nightmare he fell and fell, cart-wheeling through empty air for what seemed an eternity, and then, with a suddenness that tore the breath from his lungs, he struck something solid. But the nightmare was not yet over, and before his senses could catch up with his body the something parted and he fell still farther, crashing through one yielding surface after another, through fingers that clawed at his face and clothing even as he hurtled beyond their grasp. He lost consciousness then, knowing even as the blackness swept over him that he would never regain it, that this at last was where it ended, at the base of a remote canyon in a wild land where he had no right being.

He awoke to find himself very much in this world. His head felt swollen with blood, for the very good reason that he was looking up at his feet, one of which was caught between two pine branches and tingling for lack of circulation, while the other dangled free. His coat was shredded from having run the gauntlet of other such branches on the way down, and his face burned from cuts and scratches received the same way.

The surface he lay on swayed like a hammock. When he tried to rise, his ankle slipped three inches and he snatched at the nearest support, which turned out to be yet another needled branch. He looked down at the river rushing some fifty feet below, and didn't repeat the attempt.

A web of interlocking branches alone separated him from his fate. Slowly, lest a sudden movement deprive him of his precarious perch, he reached his right hand across his chest and groped at the wound in his left shoulder. He found to his relief that the fall had dislodged the knife and that the hole wasn't very deep. The padded canvas of his jacket had absorbed most of the impact. He had lost a substantial amount of blood, however, and his weakness concerned him along with the possibility of infection.

But those were worries that could wait until he was on solid ground. He had set about seeing what he could do to realize that goal when two men came to gaze down at him from the ledge he had just left.

His initial reaction was to hail them, but the shout lodged in his throat when he saw the tall crown of a black hat outlined against the blue of the sky. The last time he had seen that hat, a bullet from North's Ballard had plucked it from Dick Lightfoot's retreating head. Fulwider had no idea who his companion was until he turned to say something to the other and the sun glinted off the steel rim of his spectacles.

## SEVENTEEN

For an agonizing moment the journalist remained still, clutching the branches on both sides while the two men scanned the canyon at their feet. He had no way of knowing if they could see him among the treetops, but in case they could he was determined to convince them that Lightfoot's knife had done for him even if the fall had not. The thought of Sam Fire Eye making sure with his Sharps carbine paralyzed him, for which he was grateful.

His thoughts were a jumble. How Fire Eye had survived last month's withering fusillade nagged at him, conjuring up images of undying monsters left behind with the nightmares of childhood. To compound matters, his foot had begun to slip a fraction of an inch at a time from between the crossed branches holding it. In his weakened condition he didn't think his grasp on the others would prevent his own weight from finishing the job Lightfoot had started. He held his breath.

The half-breeds were withdrawing from the edge when his foot came loose.

The branch in his right hand held him for an instant, then parted. Releasing the broken piece, he clung with both hands to the limb on the other side and felt again that nightmarish sensation of hurtling movement as he swung, swung sickeningly through space and then, with a jolt that nearly wrenched his arms from their sockets, stopped, suspended twenty feet above the ground by a brittle cable the circumference of his thumb.

He let out his breath shallowly, sucked for air and felt a sharp, agonizing pinch in his right side. It was his first indication that he had injured a rib, possibly two. He hoped they weren't cracked.

The limb was creaking ominously. Slowly, his heart hammering, he uncurled the fingers of one hand from around it and began lowering himself hand over hand. Twice he stopped, breathless, when the wood split with a noise like a pistol shot and he dropped another foot. Then he resumed his descent more cautiously. At last he reached the end, only to find his feet still dangling five yards above the bank of the river. He was contemplating the chances of a successful leap when the limb made the decision for him. There was a long, peeling crackle and he was in space once again.

He had just time enough to let go of the useless branch and twist to keep from striking on his fragile right side, and then he hit the ground feet first with a force that drove his knees hard into his chest and rolled. He heard his own grunts as he hurtled along the ground out of control. When at last he came to rest he was lying face down in a tangle of rocks and branches with one hand dangling in the swift, icy waters of the river. His injured shoulder throbbed and the pain in his side was so sharp he feared that he had rammed a jagged edge of broken rib into a lung.

He lay still for he knew not how long, waiting for his breathing and heartbeat to return to normal and half expecting them to stop altogether. Then he marshaled his strength, placed his hands beneath him, pushed himself to his knees and, with the support of a dead cottonwood nearby, pulled himself upright. Nothing seemed broken. Though his right ankle was twisted and he was now certain that he had at least bruised two ribs, he could boast that he had survived a drop of two hundred feet.

If he lived long enough.

With a start he remembered the half-breeds and limped for cover into the canyon's wooded fringe, squinting through the treetops to see if anyone was watching from above. He couldn't tell, and had no way of determining if the noise of his descent had alerted them. Finally he gave up looking and hobbled back to the river.

There he bathed his lacerated face and stripped off his shredded jacket and shirt to get at his shoulder. He cleansed the wound as thoroughly as he could with his soaked kerchief and applied an awkward pad bandage jury-rigged from the tail of his shirt to keep out infection. It occurred to him as he did so that since coming west he had grown adept at crude frontier first aid. He then applied a cold compress to ease the pain in his side and tested it with probing fingers to assure himself that the rib cage was indeed just knocked about and not fractured or broken. Dressing carefully, he considered examining his hurt ankle, then vetoed it for fear of not being able to get the boot back on.

His exertions had taken their toll, and for a long time he sat there, literally too weak to move. But for miscellaneous minor injuries and a general sensation of having been trampled under a herd of healthy bison, he had passed through a harrowing episode relatively unscathed. Yet he was far from elated. That he had used up his allotted miracle, and was living on borrowed time from now on was not a pleasant thought. His only consolation was that Sam Fire Eye was in similar straits after sustaining enough gunshot wounds delivered at close range to destroy a small army and living to tell the story.

At that point, Fulwider stopped thinking about himself. For if, as he hoped, the killers believed him to have been dealt with, they would now seek to settle their account with Asa North.

The journalist was hardly in a position to stop them. On foot, weaponless and without supplies, he was as much at the mercy of nature as he had been at Lightfoot's lack of it. His wisest course was to return to Rebellion. Without a horse it would be a week's journey, but that was preferable to following the half-breeds on North's trail, in which case he would face death on two counts, from lack of the materials necessary for survival and from Lightfoot and Fire Eye themselves. Sanity demanded that he go back to town.

He chose to follow the half-breeds. Had he been sane he would never have selected journalism as a vocation in the first place.

Believing at first that a crutch would slow him down, he endeavored to make his way without one. But after a hundred yards his ankle began to throb, and when it showed signs of swelling he stopped and used his pocket knife to fashion a support from a forked maple limb. To his surprise, once he got the hang of it he found that he could make better time with the crutch than without it, and by this means he followed the upward slope of the bank and regained the ledge by nightfall.

He stood unmoving as the last traces of sunlight withdrew beyond the peaks to the east, listening for footsteps or whispers that would betray the presence of others. He heard none, and soon grew tired of waiting.

He selected a fairly broad spot littered with pine needles, swept the latter with the side of his good foot into a mattress of sorts, and hugging his coat about him against the spring chill, bedded down for the night. Almost immediately his stomach began to rumble. He regretted having declined breakfast, as he had vomited up most of what he had eaten the evening before and it had now been nearly thirty-six hours since he had enjoyed a decent meal. But his exhaustion was greater than his hunger, and even his fear of discovery by the enemy couldn't prevent sleep from overtaking him.

His dreamless state was interrupted only once. He sat up, certain he had heard something. It echoed in his head as an eerie, drawn-out wail, oddly human. Wondering grumpily when he would get used to the sound of wolves howling, he turned up his collar and dropped back into unconsciousness.

The sun was in his eyes when he came to himself. Immediately he started coughing, white-hot pain ripping his side. When it was over he felt drained and the urge to drink was greater than the urge to live. There were flecks of blood in his handkerchief. In the light of day he wondered what had possessed him to choose this course instead of the safety of civilization. But he had come too far now to turn back.

He groped blindly to his feet, put too much weight on his swollen right ankle and clutched at the clammy stone of the canyon wall to keep from falling. His crutch leaned nearby. He fumbled it under his arm and began swinging his way deeper into the Caribou Mountains, coughing with each step.

He hadn't gone half a mile when something crunched against stone up ahead.

He flattened against the wall. The noise had come from the other side of a long bend. He waited five minutes, but when no one appeared he inched his way forward, one hand gripping the crutch that represented his only weapon.

Moments later, the sound was repeated, accompanied by a drawn groan, as of the creaking of a ship's rigging in rough seas. Again he stopped, waited. Again no one showed himself. He lifted a stone the size of an egg from a small pile of rubble on the ledge and cast it around the bend, hugging the wall as it struck the edge and fell clattering to the canyon bottom.

There was no reaction. After another minute he squared his shoulders and stepped boldly out into the open, muscles primed for self-defense or retreat.

Jim Stemmer hung from a rope tied to a tree at the top of the wall, twisting slightly as the wind caught him and dragged his boots against the stone. His eyes and tongue protruded and his face was the color of the dark iron that streaked this side of the canyon.

# EIGHTEEN

Fulwider was no tracker, and yet the signs were easily enough read if he dared to believe them.

The young wolfer's shirt was open, exposing more than a dozen ugly brown sores as large as dimes on his chest and stomach, such as might have been made by the glowing tip of a cigar. The sour smell of burned flesh was thick in the air. Nearby lay a small conical boulder, mossy side down.

Lightfoot and Fire Eye had waylaid Jim on his way to town with the first load of skins, strung him up and erected the boulder so that he balanced on top of it between life and death. They had proceeded to torture him into disclosing the whereabouts of Asa North and his brother. Once they had obtained that information they had kicked away his support and left him to strangle. All this had taken place last night, for his flesh was cold to the touch.

The journalist peered over the edge. He couldn't see for the trees, but it was probable that the half-breeds had run Jim's mount and pack horse into eternity on the banks of the river far below to prevent them from wandering and spreading curiosity. Perhaps Fulwider's gray had shared their fate, or been claimed as spoils. He remembered the wail he had attributed to wolves last night and wondered if it had been the horses' screams he had heard or Stemmer's cries of agony.

Fighting back nausea, he set up the boulder and climbed on top to cut down the remains. They flopped to the rocky surface like a sack of laundry. For a long moment he stood staring down at the corpse, and then he grabbed a handful of Jim's collar and dragged it one-handed to the edge. Balancing on the crutch, he pushed it on over. There was a short silence after it finished crashing through the trees, followed by a distant splash. That was better than he'd hoped, for there was a chance that someone would discover the body downriver and send help.

The deed done, Fulwider lowered himself to the ledge and spent several minutes dry-retching into the canyon.

The rest of that day and the following night dropped through a ragged hole in his memory. Shaggy and unshaven, his emaciated figure draped in rags, he stumped on his rustic crutch through flashes of delirium and lucidity, aware only of his pain and the next step and then the next. He had a vague impression of curling up for another night on a bed of green moss in a hollowed-out section of wall, but entertained no clear thought until the next morning, when he found himself deep in the mountains. He shielded his eyes against the bright sun with a hand filthy with moss and dirt and bits of bark from the crutch. His stomach seemed to brush his backbone with every breath and something was crawling under the bandage on his shoulder, but he was afraid to look and see the maggots.

He tested his weight on the twisted ankle. It seemed to be holding. Briefly he considered the forked limb, then flung it as far across the canyon as he could manage. It began its descent ten feet short of the opposite wall, twisting and flipping end over end for a long time before vanishing in a white smear into the river.

He started climbing, dragging himself hand over hand up the rocky incline over which he and North and Dale Crippen had coaxed their horses in another lifetime. He tore his hands on the craggy surface and wore his trousers through at the knees, but he continued scaling. Once he placed his hand inside a slot between rocks and something scurried over it on its way out. He snatched at it, catching it by its stubby tail. A ground squirrel. He wrung its neck and devoured it, bones, intestines and all.

Fortified by his first meal in three days, he continued to the summit and pulled himself onto the plateau where so much had happened since his journey west. There he rested, stretched out on his stomach in the tall grass. After an hour he rose and stumbled onward. Night was falling when he reached the base of the mountain and the wolf's den.

The ravens should have prepared him for what he found. He had spotted them upon reaching the level, wheeling and diving in the scraped blue sky over the peaks, but he had assumed they were feeding on the carcasses of the slain wolves. What was left of Aaron Stemmer when with squawking fanfare the curtain of flapping black wings was lifted made his stomach lurch.

He had been camped when the killers came upon him, and probably sleeping. That explained the charred remains of a fire, long since extinguished, and the fact that he was still wrapped, more or less, in his blanket. It had been all but dragged off by wolves, coyotes and the ubiquitous ravens in a feeding frenzy.

A shuddering snort behind him brought Fulwider around in a crouch. Startled, the bay gelding he remembered from the pack string backed up and rolled its wall-eye. The animal was contrary by nature, and could be expected to return after having been run off by the half-breeds. Fulwider relaxed.

Missing along with the other horses were Aaron's Winchester carbine and Colt revolver, and Asa North. Lightfoot and Fire Eye would have confiscated the firearms, and North would have been well up the mountainside when they struck the camp, having laid his plans to keep moving while the Stemmers took charge of skinning and transporting.

A brief search uncovered Jim Stemmer's rifle, an ancient cap-and-ball affair with an overlong barrel bound in brass, abandoned in the weeds. Evidently they had taken it from him over the river and discarded it in favor of his brother's more modern weaponry. It had been fired.

"Whoa, boy." Repeating it over and over soothingly, Fulwider worked his way toward the skittish horse. The animal tossed back its head and shied away. He stopped.

A full moon had risen, throwing his shadow across the beast's forefeet. Snorting, it danced away from the long black thing that appeared to be reaching for it. The journalist noted this and circled around slowly until he was facing the moon. The horse pivoted to keep him in sight. He advanced with a nonchalant gait.

When the distance closed to eight feet he leaped, grasping a double handful of mane. The animal whinnied and tried to rear, but he got a hand on the harness that secured the packs to its back and dug in his heels, releasing the other hand to stroke its long neck. They waltzed around like that for two or three minutes. At length the horse settled down, reacting to the gentle stroking. It blew out its nostrils contentedly.

Fulwider untangled the leather halter and tethered the bay to a low bush. With shaking hands he opened the bundles and took out tin after tin of sardines and peaches, slabs of bacon and salt pork, sacks of coffee and boxes of matches.

Immediately he unwound one of the sardine containers and scooped the oily fish into his mouth. Aaron Stemmer was forgotten. He opened three tins in all, ate what was inside and drank off the juice. It tasted even better than the stewed beef with a fancy French name he and his fellow reporters had consumed in Commodore Vanderbilt's kitchen while covering the 1873 crash.

Suddenly he was seized with violent cramps. Before he could move from the spot he doubled over and threw up every bite. Later, when his stomach was feeling better, he got out two more tins and ate the contents more slowly, and those he kept down. Afterward he built a fire, finished unloading the horse and lay down on his good side for a restful night scant yards away from the corpse of his former companion.

In the morning he buried Aaron in a shallow grave scratched out of the ground with a knife from the packs and fixed himself a breakfast of hot, spitting bacon over the fire. He tried not to think about the things crawling under the bandage on his shoulder, for to examine the wound under those circumstances might shock him into giving up. Upon inspecting the rest of the bundles he was delighted to find a chamois leather sack containing five leaden balls, a leathern square perforated to hold three rows of brass caps and a smaller sack of the same tough material full of black powder.

Fulwider had served with the Army of the Potomac. Though the only action he saw as a company clerk in Rhode Island had to do with a heated correspondence between himself and a quartermaster sergeant at Fort Leavenworth over a shipment of flannel underwear issued in response to a requisition for twelve cases of new Springfield rifles, he had been trained in the use of muzzle-loading firearms. Making use of this fading knowledge, he loaded the rifle with a ball and probably too much powder (which he regarded as preferable to too little), wadded it with a piece of shirttail, tamped it all down with a stick and finally fitted a cap to the steel nipple under the hammer.

He stashed the rest of the equipment in a coat pocket, threw Aaron's saddle onto the gelding, filled the pouches with provisions and mounted, cradling the rifle across the worn pommel.

He now had supplies, transportation and a weapon, and for the first time in days he was once again a hunter.

The approach to the mountain, while steep, offered little difficulty as it wound laterally through the thickening cover along an old game trail worn six inches deep by the tread of thousands of hoofs. The weather was far less cooperative. Metal-colored clouds rolled in shortly after noon, and long before dusk the sky grew dark while an unseasonable gale blasted down from the peak, squeezing drops of icy rain from the overcast and dashing them like iron pellets against the journalist's face. It was as if he were being warned to stay away.

But Fulwider read a different meaning into it. In spite of his discomfort he welcomed the wind and rain, as it drowned out whatever noise he made and decreased his chances of detection by the dangerous men he was following. A lifelong believer in fate, he read the inclement weather as an omen of encouragement.

Unfortunately, his abilities did not match his optimism. No tracker, he had not the eye to study broken twigs or bent blades of grass and learn from them what direction his quarry had gone and how long ago. As for those tracks that were visible, he was at a loss to know which belonged to North's roan and which to his pack animal or the mounts of his pursuers. Though he was canny enough to distinguish an old track from a fresh one by the extent to which weather had softened the edges, the art of breaking down that erosion into terms of hours remained a mystery. He resolved to proceed with caution and play the cards as they were dealt.

With the approach of darkness he began looking for a place to camp. Just as he found a good spot he glimpsed a bright splash of yellow farther up the mountain. He was moving at the time and it vanished quickly. Uncertain that he had seen anything at all, he urged his exhausted mount ahead until it came back into view. He drew rein and sat watching it. It wavered slightly. A flame, then.

His first chilling thought was that it was a torch, with which the half-breeds proposed to continue their grim hunt throughout the night. But soon he realized that it was stationary. Whether the campfire belonged to friend or foe was the crux.

Not trusting his horsemanship, he swung down and approached the beacon on foot, leading the bay. His ankle still slowed him down, but by placing the foot firmly and carefully he could depend on its support. Still, the journey was all uphill, and he paused frequently to catch his breath and to slow his racing pulse. Despite the cold, his clothes were soon soaked through with sweat.

The horse smelled wood smoke and snorted. Quickly Fulwider cupped a hand over its nostrils. He heard camp sounds close by: A pot clanking against a tin cup, coffee hissing on the edge of the fire, wood splitting from the heat in the center. When it became evident that no one was coming to investigate the noise his horse had made, he tethered it upwind of the fire, stepped through a tangle of brush and found himself without warning in the enemy camp.

# NINETEEN

He cringed.

He hadn't thought he was that close. One moment he was sliding through thick undergrowth, one elbow cocked in front of his face to protect his eyes from thorns, and the next he was standing in a narrow alley that swooped down between stands of birch and pine to a level spot in which two men, one seated, one standing, faced each other across a banked fire. For a terrifying moment he was transfixed to the spot. Then he found his legs and drew back into the protection of the brush.

No shouts arose from camp, or if they did they were muffled by Fulwider's own heartbeat and the wind that buffeted his ears. Deprived of his night vision by the firelight, he staggered groping for his mount.

The sight was emblazoned on his memory. The seated man, wrapped in a blanket, had appeared asleep with his back propped against a tree and a rifle across his lap. The other, unmistakeably Dick Lightfoot, had been standing on the very edge of the firelight and staring, or so it seemed, straight at the intruder.

He didn't wait to find out for sure, but straddled his horse and quit the scene as fast as he dared in the darkness.

After he had gone some three hundred yards he stopped and listened, but was unable because of the wind to hear if anyone was following. Nevertheless he didn't press on. Clouds obscured the moon, and though he had heard remarkable things about Indians, the ability to see in the dark wasn't among them. In any case he was unwilling to risk his horse stepping in a hole and killing both of them. He sat and listened and thought.

If he hadn't been seen, he had a rare opportunity to dispose of the killers. In the firelight, Dick Lightfoot had offered a tempting target for his newly acquired rifle, and although he was rusty at it, he was fairly certain that if prepared he could reload and shoot Sam Fire Eye before he had wits enough about him to fight back or flee. If the situation were reversed, neither would show him any more consideration. And yet he didn't follow up his plan.

Fulwider was no murderer. He felt justified now, but knew that when the time came he wouldn't find it in him to slay two men in cold blood. That his would-be victims labored under no such restrictions was beside the point.

His one recourse was to warn North. But where was he? If he had indeed left camp before the half-breeds struck, he could be wandering anywhere about the mountain, unaware that he was being followed. If he was aware, he'd be even harder to find, but in that case there would hardly be reason to inform him of his predicament. Mulling over the paradox, Fulwider decided that he still wasn't thinking straight and wondered if his wound had mortified and the poison was fouling his brain.

Whatever his situation, it would be foolhardy to attempt to locate North's camp in this blackness. He planned instead to circle around the killers and make his own camp farther up the mountainside, where he would wait for first light and with luck be moving again before they resumed tracking. That meant staying awake all night long, but a man who had survived a plunge of two hundred feet was capable of anything.

Half a mile above the killers' berth he selected a shallow grade that rose gently through a copse of birch far enough off the game trail, he hoped, to conceal him in the event they arose first. He climbed down to unsaddle the bay.

In a fraction of a second he was torn off his feet and hurled like an enemy banner to the ground, his lungs emptying on impact with a tremendous *woof*. Fiery pain seized his injured shoulder. Fighting back unconsciousness, with the lightning reflex of blind panic he immediately rolled over onto his back, and was immediately pinned between two powerful thighs. A callused fist grasped his hair, forced his head backward until his spine creaked and a point of cold fire bit into the tender flesh of his jaw.

He felt warm mist on his face, smelled the stale odor of spent breath.

"Now I reckon we'll see what color you breeds bleed," panted a familiar voice.

Recognizing it, Fulwider gathered all his strength for a terrific shout, but when North's name came out it was in a hoarse croak, barely audible. The blade was already sliding down toward his throat. Something warm and wet trickled down the side of his neck into his collar. Suddenly the point was withdrawn, accompanied by a whispered oath.

"What the hell you doing alive?" demanded the wolfer then. He was straddling the journalist on his knees, a solid presence in the blackness. "I figured them breeds done for you like they done for Aaron."

Fulwider propped himself up on one shaky elbow and massaged his neck with his free hand, smearing the blood. His shoulder felt sticky under the bandage. The activity had torn the wound open. It throbbed like a toothache. "You know about him?'' A whisper was as much as he could manage.

Something stirred the bushes nearby. North was silent for a moment, listening. When no more sounds followed he resumed, keeping his voice low.

''I heard a shot. I didn't think it was Aaron potting at a squirrel in the middle of the night. When I spotted them breeds dogging my trail yesterday, I knowed what had happened right enough.''

''Jim's dead too.'' The journalist described the scene over the river. North grunted.

''I always knowed them boys wasn't born to die in bed.''

The blood on Fulwider's neck continued running, more profusely than seemed possible from so tiny a hole. He untied his kerchief and held it against the cut. ''May I get up?''

''I like you right where you are.''

North stiffened audibly. This was a new voice. He twisted around and half rose, clothes rustling as he reached back with one hand for the knife he had returned to its sheath. He froze when something that shone dully in the starlight breaking through the cloud cover touched his chest with a firm thump. Fulwider sensed rather than saw that there was another man standing next to the one with the gun.

''Well, Dick,'' said the voice, ''I guess you wasn't seeing things after all.'' It was the man with the gun who spoke, in a high-pitched drawl the journalist would have recognized anywhere. ''Give us some light and let's see what we got here.''

# TWENTY

A match was struck, and flame spread with a sucking sound over the head of a torch in the second man's hand to cast a ghostly, wildly flickering glow over the tiny clearing. Dick Lightfoot's grave features sprang into view dominated by the black, non-reflecting eyes Fulwider had first taken note of weeks ago in Rebellion.

He wore the black hat down to his eyes, a ragged hole showing in its crown where North's bullet had passed through it the month before. A fur vest hung over a patched and faded calico shirt, the latter's tail thrust carelessly inside the band of his breechclout and buckskin leggings. He had Fulwider's Remington rifle in one hand and Aaron Stemmer's Winchester in the other.

Unwillingly, the journalist swung his gaze from Lightfoot to his companion, and recoiled from the sight.

Sam Fire Eye had survived his multiple wounds at a fearsome cost. A bullet had smashed into his left cheek, pulverizing the bone and caving in that side of his face. His left eye was glazed over white behind the shattered lens of his spectacles. He wore his greasy derby tipped far over on that side, as if to conceal it or to protect the damaged eye from the light.

He balanced his Sharps' carbine on his left forearm. His right hung limp and evidently useless below his thin waist, the sleeve of his buffalo coat stained brown in places where the blood had soaked through long ago, as it had through the front of his shirt.

"Pretty, ain't I?" He leered lopsidedly, showing his iron teeth. "I might could get a job modeling long johns for Sears and Roebuck."

He spoke slowly, with many pauses to catch his breath. Fulwider was aware of a whistling, sucking noise increasing and diminishing, increasing and diminishing, as of the pumping of a broken bellows. It reminded him of the breathing of the mother wolf North had put out of its misery at the den, and he wondered how the half-breed had managed to live this long with a collapsed lung.

The torch was thrust butt-first into the ground, where the flame danced crazily in the gusty wind, illuminating first this face, then that as another long silence stretched to the bursting point. Once again, it was Fire Eye who pricked it.

"Where is that son-of-a-bitch cowboy? Tell me he ain't dead. Please tell me that." His tone was thin with hatred.

North didn't reply. Fulwider said, "He is. Lightfoot's knife killed him."

There was another pause, after which the half-breed released a string of curses lasting a full minute. Dizzy for want of breath, he staggered and clutched at the torch for support. His narrow face was slick with sweat. He filled his good lung and seemed about to continue when he let it out slowly.

"That's too bad," he said quietly. "For you. I can't figure why you ain't stone dead after that fall you took, tenderfoot, and I don't much care. But you'll pray to God that you was soon enough."

"I can't imagine why you're not dead yourself." Fulwider spoke to conceal his fear.

"Who made the headboard?"

North's question was so irrelevant that for a moment no one moved or spoke.

Fire Eye obliged him. "Made it myself, couple of weeks back. I figured someone would be suspicious if they didn't find no bones. Dick can't write so I done the carving. Did you like that part about not being able to find the skull? I figured that would sound real. I seen a marker like it once outside Billings."

While the other was holding forth, Fulwider cast a furtive glance about the circle of torchlight and noticed his bedroll lying where it had come loose when North knocked him down. From time to time as the wind rose and fell, the flame painted a pale stripe along the oiled stock of Jim Stemmer's long rifle protruding from the blanket in which he had wrapped it when the rain started. If either of the half-breeds had noticed it, maybe he considered the weapon harmless after having fired it and threw away what he thought was Jim's entire supply of powder and shot. It was just beyond the journalist's reach.

He played for time. "How did you survive? We left you for dead."

"Which is what I would of been except for Dick, here." Fire Eye nudged his silent companion. "That Cheyenne medicine ain't half bad when you can't get no real doctor. He says I hollered blue hell when he dug out what bullets he could with his spare knife. I don't rightly recollect. He tells me I was dead out and raving crazy mad for full ten days. I disremember that too. But I remember every step I taken since, and every time I suck wind I remember. I figure the reason I'm still breathing is I kept hoping on doing the same for Crippen's memory." Air squealed in and out of his sunken chest. "Now I guess I got to be content with you two."

The raw emotion in his labored words made the flesh crawl along Fulwider's spine. He fought to keep his gaze from returning to the bedroll and rifle for fear of drawing their attention to it. But it wandered there against all his efforts, and on the way back his eyes met North's.

The wolfer knew. Instantly they broke contact, but not before Fulwider caught the other's unspoken message: Delay.

"He must value your partnership, to take so much trouble," he told Fire Eye.

The half-breed laughed, a short, harsh bark, distinctly unpleasant. "Dick? Hell, he would have me skinned and cured by sunup if it would bring a bounty and he didn't need me. Look at him. See how my saying it makes his eyes light up?"

Fulwider looked. The Cheyenne-reared killer's expression was stony as ever, the eyes murky and bottomless. But he could sense a savage mind working behind the stoic façade.

"He saved your life."

"Like I said, he needs me. He can track a silverback across a clean sheet and he can skin a carcass in less time than it takes to tell him to, but he can't do figures. Wasn't for me, them bastards in the Stockmen's Association would take his skins and leave him with ten cents on the dollar. I ain't the only wolfer around can cipher, but no one else will ride with him. He kilt his last two partners."

Lightfoot made a noise that was very nearly a growl. Fire Eye giggled.

"All right, just the first one. The other fell off a cliff. He says. Anyway, none of the money Dick got for the hides went to his widow."

"I don't imagine we have much more to look forward to than that." The journalist was running out of conversation.

"We might," said Fire Eye. "Then again we might not. Not till you help us find Black Jack, anyway."

Fulwider stared. "You can't still be thinking about him!"

"How come?" North asked the half-breed. "You said yourself Lightfoot can track."

"If he was half the wolfer they claim you are, we would of took that bounty months ago. You got interrupted last time, but there ain't a tinhorn in Idaho would give me odds against you running him to ground this trip. I'd sort of like to be around when that happens."

"What good would it do?" pressed Fulwider. "You're both wanted for murder. Who would collect on the hide?"

The malicious gleam sharpened in Sam's good eye. "That's one more good reason to keep you kicking, ain't it? We hold onto your friend whilst you go after the money."

"Don't see much percentage in it." North retained the ready crouch he had assumed upon first hearing Fire Eye's voice, his moccasined feet planted far apart. "Since you'll just kill us as soon as he brings it back, why don't we just save time and get it all done here and now?"

"You'll help, all right. As long as we decide to let you live you'll do what we say. I might not be in your class as a wolfer, but I been one long enough to know there's one thing men and animals will do anything to hold on to, and that's their skins. Let's go, Dick. Get his knife and gun and bring them along." He turned.

North executed a spectacular leap, coming down on his right shoulder and rolling beyond the firelight. Lightfoot raised the Remington, but Fulwider kicked at the barrel and the blue flame spurted two feet off course, narrowly missing Fire Eye as he swung the Sharps around. Meanwhile North snatched up Jim Stemmer's venerable weapon and fired without bothering to pull it free of the bedroll. Raw flame obliterated the darkness. Bits of wool fiber swirled about like angry mosquitoes. Fulwider heard the heavy ball strike Sam Fire Eye with a hollow plop. He arched backward, but the journalist didn't see him fall, for by that time he and Lightfoot were grappling for the Remington.

Fulwider had grasped it while the other was reloading and been yanked to his feet as he attempted to wrest it away. They collided, went down in a tangle of arms and legs and rolled. A bolt of pain raked through the easterner from shoulder to ribs. He grimaced and tried to ignore it.

The half-breed worked one hand free and closed his fingers around the other's throat. Soon they became slippery with blood—Fulwider's, still leaking from the wound North had opened in his neck. But he held on. Every cell in the journalist's body screamed for oxygen. His vision retreated behind a curtain of purple. He felt his own fingers slipping from the rifle when suddenly the pressure was released.

His senses came swarming back. He was alone on the ground, still clutching the Remington. Dick Lightfoot stood in front of him in the wavering illumination of the torch, staring beyond Fulwider's shoulder. The latter swung his head in that direction and saw North crouched half in shadow pointing the long rifle, empty now, at the half-breed. That it was empty seemed to occur to Lightfoot at the same moment, for he turned and fled into the darkness.

"Shoot him!" shouted the wolfer. "Remember what happened last time!"

The luxury of deciding whether to commit murder was no longer the journalist's. Later he wouldn't remember if it even crossed his mind at the time. Automatically, as if from long practice, he snugged the butt of the big rifle against his shoulder, drew a swift bead on Lightfoot's dim back and pressed the trigger. The weapon pulsed against his shoulder and the running figure dropped from sight.

The roar echoed crackling in the distance for what seemed an impossible length of time.

"Did I hit him?" The voice was Fulwider's, and yet he listened to it as if it belonged to a third party. He staggered to his feet, the rifle drooping. He felt more drained than he had in the face of starvation.

"Dead center." A hand gripped the rifle. Tardily, for his fingers were still responding to the message to hold on at all costs, he released it to North's care.

As in the final moments of a restless dream, the images flashed past too rapidly to follow. The wolfer approached Sam Fire Eye's prostrate body, spread-eagled with one knee cocked in the air. Fulwider smelled cooking flesh and saw that the front of the half-breed's shirt was in flames from the muzzle-loader's flash. North reloaded the Remington from a handful of cartridges he had taken from the journalist's pocket without his knowledge. Muttering something about taking no chances this time, he placed the snout of the rifle against Sam's head.

The report was hard and flat, like a dog's warning bark. Without pausing he strode past his partner in the direction of Dick Lightfoot's aborted retreat, reloading as he went.

Fulwider didn't hear the second shot. As if a valve had been thrown open in his system, he felt his remaining strength rushing down the calves of his legs and he slid into a cauldron of whirling black and very bright scarlet.

## TWENTY-ONE

"**D**rink this."

He was lying on a bed of damp, fibrous material, and for a frightening moment he believed that he was back in the canyon, depending for his life on a fragile network of pine branches. Then the words registered and he realized that the something supporting the back of his head was the palm of a man's hand. Its mate, brown and hard and corded, with thick, square nails, held a tin cup to his lips from the depths of which warm vapor welled up into his nostrils smelling of heat and coffee and something else even more welcome. He drank. The liquid scalded his tongue and burned a raw furrow down his throat. It was sheer luxury.

As the familiar warmth spread through him his senses cleared. His mattress was a layer of pine needles, and he was being toasted on one side by a fire so hot the enameled pot from which his coffee had been poured stood steaming on a flat rock placed nearly two feet from the flames. Directly in front of him, so near it filled his vision when he looked in that direction, hovered Asa North's face, weathered beyond its years, his lupine eyes regarding Fulwider's from the shadow of his hat brim. So far as his expression could be read, he appeared concerned. There the other's gaze ceased to wander. He knew now where he was, and there were things in that clearing he didn't want to see.

North tipped the cup toward him a second time. He shook his head, only then noticing the wadded obstruction under his right ear.

"No more coffee." It came out in a hoarse whisper. He cleared his throat. "But if I tasted what I think I tasted, you might give me some more of that."

The wolfer grunted, set down the cup and picked up a flat metal flask from the ground. The strong smell of fermented grain seized Fulwider's nostrils as he pushed it near, filling his limbs with strength. He accepted it and tipped it up, letting the heady liquid slide over his tongue. The years fell away like scales. Reluctantly he handed back the vessel.

His head was lowered to an object that turned out to be Aaron Stemmer's saddle and the hand was withdrawn. He touched the lump on his neck with a tentative finger. It was a ball of fabric secured by a ragged ribbon of similar material tied around his neck. As he lowered his hand he felt a new stiffness in the opposite shoulder.

"Leave that where it is for now," North said. "I nicked the vein."

"You shaved me." His voice was coming back.

"Had to, to get at the cut. It weren't easy with just my knife. You looked like a mountain man I knowed in Montana. He lived on raw meat washed down with warm blood."

"My shoulder."

"I cleaned it good and dressed it up proper. You may not take to it, but you owe your life to a bunch of maggots. They eaten away the rotten part and kept the poison out of your blood. I suppose you got Lightfoot to thank for that."

He nodded, and noticed for the first time that the sky

was growing pale. He felt that rush of panic that accompanies the fear of having slept through a large chunk of one's life. "How long have I been unconscious?"

"Couple of hours. You was pale as a gnawed bone when I drug you over here. I had you down for dead."

Something crackled when Fulwider moved. He glanced down and saw that the front of his shirt was caked with dried blood. It made him think of Sam Fire Eye and Dick Lightfoot. "Are they both dead?"

"If they get up, listen for the horn."

Nausea gripped his vitals. But for the lone wolf last month, the journalist had never before killed a living thing. He tried to convince himself that North's final bullet in Lightfoot's head had done the job, but it didn't work.

He started to climb to his feet. North made no attempt to stop him. A moment later he knew why. He fell back, feeling sapped. The strength he thought he'd regained had come directly from the flask.

"A man's like a wolf some ways," said the other placidly. "They can both get by without food nor sleep a lot longer than anyone says they can. But take away their blood and they're meat for ravens."

"Like those half-breeds?" He chafed at North's complacence. "I hardly imagine that you buried them."

His eyebrows went up slightly. "Did they bury the Stemmers?"

"Then we're no better than they were."

"Never said I was. Just different."

The journalist hadn't the energy to press the point. For a time he lay still, listening to his breathing grow steady—listening, or so he fancied, to his blood replacing itself slowly, slowly. He asked North his plans.

"To hunt wolves."

"Now?" His heart resumed racing. Like any powerful

pump more than adequate for the minimal amount of fluid it was charged to circulate, it accelerated on the least provocation. He forced himself to relax. "What about all that's happened? There must be someone to notify, some authority."

It may have been a trick played by the firelight, but in that moment it seemed that a smile touched the wolfer's features. "You mean Oscar Adamson?"

Fulwider nodded, conscious suddenly of how far he was from home. "If we're still in his jurisdiction."

"Go home, New York."

The other looked at him. He was studying his reflection in his knife's polished blade, stroking with a stiff forefinger the sandy stubble that peppered his cheeks and chin.

"You draw my origins as if they were weapons against me. A man can't help where he comes from."

"He can't help what he is, neither." The whiskers made scraping sounds under his finger.

"Why do you hunt wolves?"

"It's what I do."

"That's no answer." Fulwider paused. "Is it because of what happened to your wife and child?"

For a tense moment, the journalist thought he was going to be attacked. North's face went bone-white and his eyes smoldered in their sockets. A tendon worked along one side of his jaw. Fulwider glanced uneasily at the knife in the wolfer's fist. That seemed to break the spell.

By degrees North relaxed into his former lethargy, and the easterner felt ashamed. Infuriated by the other's manner, he had wanted to hurt him and was appalled at his success.

"Please accept my apology."

North said nothing. Fulwider retreated behind the clinical mask of the professional newspaperman.

"I'm merely curious about your motives. Are you like a

wolfer I met in town, who considers the animal a menace
to be eradicated?''

The knife was slid into its worn sheath. When he spoke,
North's tone was as bland as his expression.

"They kill to eat, just like you and me. Or did, until we
got spoilt. Before we come they kilt buffalo. Now the buffalo's gone and they kill cattle. It stumps me why everyone's so surprised.''

"But they couldn't have killed as many bison as they
have cattle. The statistics are appalling.''

"You're right there. Back then we done all the killing.
With all them buffalo carcasses left out there to rot, it ain't
hard to calculate why the wolf population taken a big leap.
Trouble is, folks think it's still growing. That's one of the
reasons why every time a cow or a bull dies, whether it's
from sickness or cold or old age, they holler wolf. Another
is that you can't fight sickness or cold or old age, but you
can kill a wolf on account of you can see him and hear him
and he's handy. Which is why I do what I do, because the
bounty's the only wages in this country that's going up.''

"Is that why you do it? For the money?''

He made a face. "Put that way, it sounds mighty low. I
reckon you newspaper fellows write stories for the pure hell
of it.''

Fulwider threw up his hands in mock surrender. The ef-
fort was almost too much for him and he let them drop.
"You admire them, don't you?'' he said. "Especially Black
Jack.''

"I know him. I know what he does and I know why he
does it. I know what he's going to do next and he knows
I know it. Out here he's smart as I am. Smarter.'' He
paused. "If all that means I admire them, then I guess I
do.''

He was growing restless. Rosy light bled into the patch

of gray sky. The journalist hastened to ask his next question while he still had the wolfer's attention.

"Why did you invite me along on this hunt? You never explained that to my satisfaction."

North rose. This placed the other at a disadvantage, for it thrust his features into the darkness and hid his expression. He was silent for so long that Fulwider was considering withdrawing the query when he answered.

"You wanted to write about wolfing," he said. "I repay my debts."

Fulwider hesitated. "After this morning, I think we can consider it repaid in full."

"Not till we get you home."

"No, I'd rather stay."

Again, seconds crawled past before North spoke. Birds greeted the dawn with cheerful, complicated little whistles that were repeated farther off without a note lost. North's horse was standing nearby, along with the bay and his pack animal and two others, one a paint, the other a sleek dun Fulwider recognized as Jim Stemmer's mount. Probably the half-breeds had confiscated it to replace the paint Fire Eye had lost last month.

"You got that kind of gumption," North said then, "you don't need me to look after you."

"Did I ask you to?"

He started saddling the roan. "You got supplies enough for a week, and I busted up enough wood for three or four fires if you don't build them too big. After that you ought to be able to do for yourself. I drug the breeds over to the edge of the mountain and tossed them over so's the stink won't trouble you. That's as much burial as they'll get from me." He yanked tight the cinch and turned to load the white-stockinged black.

"You knew I'd decide to stay, didn't you?" accused the

other. "You didn't just happen to make those arrangements for my comfort."

North said nothing. The pack horse grunted as the straps were secured.

"Will you be back this way?" Fulwider asked.

"Don't worry, you'll get your cut of the bounty."

"That isn't what I was concerned about, and you know it."

He gave the tracks a trial push. The bonds held. Then he stripped the two extra horses of saddles and bridles and handed each a smart slap on the rump. They whinnied indignantly and galloped off in different directions.

"Come after me if you want, when you feel up to it," said the wolfer. "One thing. When you get close—"

"I know," said Fulwider, and grinned weakly. "Make a lot of noise."

For an hour after North disappeared into the brush higher up the mountain, the journalist lay unmoving. When it became obvious that in spite of his weakness he wouldn't fall asleep, he set about rebuilding the smoldering fire, resting after each piece of wood was in place. Another twenty minutes passed in this fashion before he laid the first of four thick slices of bacon carved off the square chunk North had left him into the cast iron skillet. The essentials had all been deposited within reach, and he was pleased to find that the coffee pot was nearly full.

He was far from hungry, but it was his studied opinion that substantial quantities of food were needed to restore what he had lost through his two wounds. The very act of chewing exhausted him. Stuffed at last, he settled back onto his bed of pine needles, and this time he slept. And dreamed.

Bizarre dreams mostly, brought on by his blood loss and

featuring people he didn't know doing things he couldn't report in print. But eventually these grew less frequent, and he found himself in familiar surroundings among acquaintances he recognized.

He saw New York City and the woman who had been his wife and the city room at the *World*, complete with Mr. Pulitzer looking professorial in his pince-nez and severe black beard. The old man was waiting impatiently, thumbs hooked inside the lapels of his frock coat, for an item from Fulwider's typewriting machine that would rescue the newspaper from some undisclosed disaster. But when the journalist tore the last page from the cylinder and made to hand it over, the publisher had vanished, to be replaced by the shattered, leering figure of Sam Fire Eye in his tilted derby and buffalo coat. Terrified, Fulwider leaped to his feet, but he wasn't fast enough to escape the roar of the deranged wolfer's Sharps pointed straight at him.

Mercifully the scene changed, and the easterner was standing on the station platform in Rebellion, gazing for the first time upon the bleak place that was to be his new home. Dale Crippen was there, as were Nelson Meredith and Aaron and Jim Stemmer, the latter pair carrying a dead she-wolf slung upside-down from a pole. The woman with whom Fulwider had spent an hour in Aurora's place was there as well, though he didn't know why. It was a placid scene, and nothing happened in it that was worth remembering when the journalist awoke.

But he was far from waking.

From there his fevered imagination went spinning down other alleys, some familiar, some fantastic, lined with wooden grave markers bearing deceptive inscriptions and strangled pups and the ravaged carcasses of animals and human corpses that swayed in the breeze or lay like bloated gray slugs in the rags of their clothing. He saw friends with

knives protruding from their backs and men forced at gun-
point to eat bloody wolf meat and men slashing other men
with knives in cramped barrooms and scenery hurtling past
as he fell, fell for leagues through empty space and black
eyes that reflected no light and broken faces behind broken
spectacles and, weaving in and out among them with an
effortless gait that belied the tremendous speed it was making, the fleeing form of a black-mantled wolf.

At length the images dissolved, and Fulwider was kneel-
ing alone in a circle of firelight in the wilderness, watching
a man's back retreating into the shadows. In response to a
voice shouting inside of him, he lifted a heavy rifle to his
shoulder, took aim at the nearly invisible target and fired.
Only this time, when the figure spun and fell, a shaft of
wind-whipped flame fell across the victim's face, revealing
not the wooden features of Dick Lightfoot, but the cadav-
erous, bearded countenance of Joseph Pulitzer.

He came awake with a start to find himself drenched with
sweat, his heart racing. Bewildered at first, he slowly grew
aware of his surroundings, and settled back by degrees. It
was some time before he realized that the shot he had heard
had not been part of his dream at all.

# TWENTY-TWO

It was the echo that alerted him, snarling among the peaks to the west, or rather the memory of it. For while it was there he had been in that twilight state in which no one can separate dream from reality. He attempted to rise, fell back when the dizziness swept over him, rested for a moment and tried again. This time he made it, only to realize that dusk was settling. Reluctantly he made sure that his bay was content with its grazing and returned to his bed to await daylight.

For some time he stayed awake, full of anxiety for North and afraid to pick up his nightmare where it had left off. But the mere effort of getting up only to lie down again had been too much, and eventually he fell comatose.

At sunrise he felt stronger than he had in days. Still, he took his time preparing breakfast, rested again afterward and then, relying on the support of a convenient spruce, pulled himself erect and leaned against the trunk while the vertigo and nausea passed. He choked back a spell of coughing. Pacing himself like an old man just back from the hospital, he faced the ordeal of saddling and lashing his remaining bundles across his horse's rump. North had reloaded his Remington and left it for him along with the extra cartridges Lightfoot had stolen from Fulwider's saddle pouch, and these he wrapped for storage in his blanket.

The bay reached back to snap at him as he was mounting, but it was a half-hearted effort, as the animal was bored and eager to return to the trail, and Fulwider ignored it. Dragging himself up and over its back required all his attention.

Four hours later he learned the reason for what he was now certain had not been Asa North's shot. Sprawled amid the undergrowth where it had come to rest, the dead wolf was so well concealed under leaves and twisting vines that his horse nearly stepped on it.

Instinctively he wrapped the reins around his wrist to take up the slack before the terrified animal could bolt. For a tense moment it danced about the carcass, blowing a keen note of fear and frustration through its nostrils, its eyes showing white. He backed it away from the twin scents of death and danger and stroked its neck until it calmed down, meanwhile examining the carcass from his high perch.

He was hardly expert enough to be able to distinguish one wolf from another at random, and yet he knew at a glance that this wasn't Black Jack. Smaller and less rangy, the beast had a coat of gunmetal gray streaked with brown and showed but one wound, a ragged opening behind its right foreleg an inch too high to have penetrated its heart. It had bled considerably before dying and had thrashed about so that it was hopelessly entangled in the serpentine growth that all but covered it. This in itself was reason enough for a wolfer in a hurry not to bother taking the skin, as that would demand several minutes of extrication before the first cut could be made. But Fulwider felt certain that this particular wolfer wouldn't have bothered in any case. He had shot the wolf out of habit; his real target still awaited his attention.

The question was, in which direction had that attention led him?

Even had the journalist been any kind of tracker, there was nothing to be gained from a study of the immediate terrain, carpeted as it was by thorny growth. Instead he took as his guide an axiom employed by the old wolfer he had interviewed in Rebellion: A pursued beast always heads for the high ground. Steering around the stiff carcass, he kicked his reluctant mount onward toward the peak.

The foliage grew thinner as they advanced. After another hour it vanished entirely, except in those spots where a single startling burst of green erupted through a fissure or a space where two rocks did not quite meet, invariably sporting a wild blossom of yellow or white or periwinkle to bob in frivolous incongruity between planes of bleak stone. At this point the bay's footing grew feeble, and he dismounted to lead it over the weather-rounded surface.

This was his first experience with mountain travel, and he was astonished to learn that the stability with which he had always associated the mighty monoliths was largely nonexistent. Millions of years of erosion and expansion had shattered the face into a thousand crevices, loosening the surface so that a single imprudent footfall was enough to send a cascade of stones roaring to the bottom, baring the succeeding layer to those same destructive elements for some future transient to upset, and so on, until in a distant millenia the mountain would be less than a memory.

Eventually, progress directly up the face grew impossible, and he set the horse's hoofs on a ledge that wound around the rocky summit. Tilting his head to catch the light, he was encouraged to see the outline of a steel shoe in the paper-thin dust that coated the surface. Even as he looked at it, the wind came up and carried part of it away in a gritty cloud. It was fresh.

The reddening sun was sliding down the conical peak of the higher mountain to the west when he came upon North's roan and black, still girded for travel, tugging at a sickle of grass in a sheltered notch. There was no sign of their master, and Fulwider felt a sudden pang of fear that in his eagerness the wolfer had forgot himself and stepped off the ledge. He looked down at the lofty pines spread out like a well-cropped lawn far below and the tendons behind his knees tingled.

He considered. The ledge was fairly broad; there seemed no reason to abandon the horses if North planned to continue along the same route. Logic suggested that he had chosen another where the horses couldn't follow. Twenty feet ahead of them a fresh-looking pile of rubble lay at the base of the wall, directly under a twisted trunk of stunted tree wedged between boulders six feet higher. It would be a simple matter to grasp the tree and begin scaling, dislodging small stones as one progressed.

Backtracking, Fulwider spotted a partial paw print in the damp alluvial soil at the bottom of a meandering gully less than twelve inches wide that carved its way up the mountainside at a gentle angle. It was ideal for the limited climbing ability of a wolf, but too narrow to admit a full-grown man in pursuit. North would have seen it quicker than the journalist, and in far less time he would have detected the animal cunning behind it, the attempt on the part of his quarry to throw him off by switching trails.

Fulwider left his bay grazing with the other horses and reached to wrap his fingers around the small tree, drawing up his legs and hanging to test its strength. He gasped at the pain in his side and shoulder and dropped back to the ledge. A few moments passed before he was willing to try again.

Much of his normal strength had returned since that

morning and yet the sweat stood out on his forehead as he braced a sole against the mountain and pulled himself up with both hands. For a space his other foot scraped at the nearly vertical surface, and then it inserted itself in a triangular abrasion where some rockfall or other had plucked a shard from the smooth granite. From there it was almost as easy as mounting a ladder.

After ten minutes he hitched himself up and over a shallow escarpment and lay there, his chest heaving. Something oozed down his back and he knew that he had once again opened the wound in his shoulder. The wadded cloth North had secured to his neck flapped loose. He stroked the thick, hard scab that had formed over the cut, tore loose the crusted cloth and cast it away. Then he got up. There was no dizziness, so he continued.

From there the way to the crest was a steep but uneven grade made up of layered rock very much like the construction of Egypt's pyramids, forming a crude staircase. Shoots of grass and similar vegetation made the going treacherous, having cracked apart the stone. Once he placed all his weight on a flat overhang and had to snatch at a handful of tough bunch grass when it tilted under his foot. It rattled down the slope and struck the ledge below the escarpment with a loud report. He hoped none of the horses had been standing in its path. Slowly he lowered himself to his most recent purchase and waited for his heart to stop thudding before he tried again.

Farther up, he heard a noise and paused.

Or he thought it was a noise. On reflection, it seemed as if he had felt it only. The impression was that of a very low sigh. The wind had died at just that moment, and he couldn't be sure that what he had heard wasn't just the whimper of its passage around the mountain. Nevertheless he began handing himself in that direction.

It was slow going. Grasping likely knobs and crevices, he tested each before proceeding, paying out inches like rope. It struck him then that he might be heading toward danger, and again he stopped to consider.

If it was Black Jack he had heard—and as he thought about it he became convinced that the sound was more animal than human—he was approaching a wounded adversary, perhaps placing himself between the animal and escape. He recalled Dale Crippen's assurance of the wolf's unwillingness to clash with man under any circumstances, but professions of that sort were easier to accept while seated before a warm campfire than while standing on a shifting platform three thousand feet in the air, a few yards away from an injured predator. He regretted having left his rifle with the horses, but he had needed both hands for climbing.

He nearly lost his footing when he continued around the curve and glimpsed gray fur within an arm's length. Rocks rolled out from under him as he hugged the mountain, breathing dust and granite. Then he perceived Asa North's angular frame under his shaggy coat. Relief pumped warmth through his veins like whiskey.

The wolfer was standing on a flat rock outcropping with his back turned to Fulwider. His shoulders sagged and the Ballard drooped at the end of his arm. He had fashioned a sling from horse tack and tied it to the weapon so that he could climb without surrendering it.

Fulwider was certain that North knew of his presence, and yet the wolfer didn't turn as he approached. All his concentration was centered on something just below him.

A rusted iron peg had been driven into the granite between his moccasined feet. Appended to it, a length of aged chain stretched taut over the edge of the outcropping. From that dangled a P-shaped device of corroded steel, clamped around the left hind leg of a great gray beast with head and shoulders as black as char.

The creature hung at full length over the green matting of forest far below, supported only by the trap. The leg thus ensnared was obviously broken. Its right shoulder was bloodied as well, but the wound was days old.

"He was running along that ridge up yonder." North spoke quietly, tipping his hat brim toward an uneven shelf twenty feet overhead. "I was drawing a bead when he leaped for this rock. I heard the snap and seen him go over."

He stopped. The wind hummed through fissures in the mountain. Then: "That trap must of been set ten, twelve years ago. The rest of the ledge has been gone at least that long. Who'd of thought it'd still work?"

A razor-thin gust came up, snapping their coattails viciously and moaning about their ears like a soul in torment. Then it died, and in the lull Fulwider heard something that gripped his heart like a cold hand. It was a whimper, soft and low and distinctly animal.

North stiffened as though struck. The two leaned out as far as they dared, watching and listening. As they did so, the trapped beast opened its black-lipped mouth and began to pant.

The wolfer wasted no time. In one smooth motion he brought the rifle scooping to the base of the wolf's skull and slammed an ounce of lead into its brain. The impact sent it swinging wildly at the end of the chain. The body jerked spasmodically, drew in upon itself, then relaxed, uncoiling by degrees. It swayed twisting in the returning wind. The chain creaked and parted with a pop.

The shaggy carcass plummeted for a thousand feet, bounded off a shelf of shale, and dropped out of sight among the pines. They kept watching for a long time after it had vanished.

"We'll never find it in all that," North said. "Even if we did, there wouldn't be nothing left of it after the varmints was through with it."

"I don't need the money anyway," put in Fulwider.

"Reckon we can both live without it." The wolfer slung his rifle over one shoulder and turned away from the edge.

# TWENTY-THREE

North and Fulwider made camp on level ground, where the wolfer redressed his partner's wound and they ate and rested for the journey back. Days later they were moving along the ledge over the river when they spotted eight horsemen crossing through the shallows. The rider in front was heavily built and had a shotgun across his saddle.

"Adamson," North observed. "Here's where we split up, New York."

Fulwider stared at him. "What for? You've done nothing to have to flee the law."

The wolfer smiled sadly, the mirth falling short of his yellow-brown eyes. "I'm like Black Jack some ways. Whenever I see a bunch of men coming in my direction, I go the other way."

"Where will you go?"

"They got this old wolf over in Wyoming they call Popeye. I hear tell he swallows cows whole and spits out the bones. Think I'll give him a try."

The journalist searched his mind for words. It infuriated him that whenever it really counted he could find none. At length he stretched out his hand. North clasped it briefly and let go. Physical contact unnerved him. He backed his horse behind Fulwider's, turned and retraced their steps up the ledge, tugging the loaded black behind. Soon they were gone behind a vertical ridge of iron-streaked stone.

At dusk, Fulwider came upon the posse at the base of the canyon. Rifles rattled. Sheriff Adamson held up a hand and the weapons were lowered. He looked businesslike in a linen duster the size of a tent, straddling a shaggy buckskin with a white blaze. The journalist reined in and waited for the group to overtake him at a walk.

"Where is North?" asked the lawman, stopping before the journalist. His small, bright eyes roamed the canyon.

"I have no idea," said the other truthfully. "We parted away back."

"You might as well tell us the truth. I have sent wires all over the territory with his description. He cannot get far."

The other horsemen were hard-eyed westerners wearing side arms and carrying rifles, some of them with scopes as long as their barrels. Fulwider recognized some of them from town.

"What is this all about?"

Adamson regarded him coolly. "Yesterday, Cal Dingle went fishing and hooked a dead man out of the river. It was Jim Stemmer, and he had a rope around his neck. What can you tell us about that?"

"He was murdered. Dick Lightfoot and Sam Fire Eye killed him."

A snicker rippled through the posse. Nothing stirred the sheriff's heavy face, however.

"Sam Fire Eye has been dead for weeks. You saw him die and I saw the grave. I am placing you under arrest." The shotgun's muzzles swung in Fulwider's direction. "John, see if he has a gun in that bedroll."

A small man with a tight, weathered face sidled his horse

alongside the journalist's, rummaged a hand inside the bound blanket and pulled out the Remington. Meanwhile, its owner stammered out a half-comprehensible account of the events of the past week. Adamson sat unblinking throughout the narrative, a living Buddha.

"We will see if North's story agrees with yours," he said, when it was finished. "Did he say where he was going?"

Fulwider shook his head. It was the first time he had ever lied to an authority, but then he had done and seen many things since leaving New York that he had never thought he would, or even dreamed were possible. He could tell that the sheriff didn't believe him.

"I am disappointed." His heavy accent was tinged with genuine sadness. "Not long ago I warned you of the dangers of falling in with wild men. They will not be civilized. Any attempt to do so brings only ruin. I hoped you understood, but I see now that you did not."

He paused, as if to give the easterner an opportunity to change his mind. When he didn't reply, the sheriff's large face hardened. "John, Fred, in the morning you will escort Mr. Fulwider back to town. See that he does not leave until we return with North." He rapped the orders out harshly, glaring at the prisoner.

"You may never return," Fulwider pointed out, "with North."

Adamson had dismounted. Others followed his lead and began preparing for camp. On foot, he lost a great deal of the authority he enjoyed in the saddle, but the glance he shot the journalist was as solid as a blow.

"You have not heard the news. The man I was looking for, who strangled Mrs. Pollard for her gold? I found him. He stood trial yesterday, and next Friday he will stand on the scaffold. They said I would not catch him, either."

It was a jovial camp. The chief tracker, a black man raised by the Sioux who worked in the livery stable between posses, sang "Laredo" in a rich bass to harmonica accompaniment, and a moustachioed cowman on loan from Newcastle Ranch told a number of humorous anecdotes from his trail-drive past while the others ate sausages and fried potatoes around a chuckling fire. Fulwider scraped his plate clean in silence and thought about what Adamson had said.

Tight-faced John manacled the journalist's hands behind his back at bedtime and settled him between himself and Fred, whose fleshy jowls and benevolent expression Fulwider recognized from behind the counter in the harness shop. He then tied one end of a six-foot length of rope to the chain and the other around his ankle, "Just in case you're fool enough to want to bust your neck wandering around them mountains with your wrists shackled." Amid coughs and whispered curses and premature snores, the posse bedded down for its first night on the trail.

Fulwider was lying on his back, staring at the stars in a clear black sky when amiable Fred hissed his name. John was snoring smoothly. The prisoner turned his head.

"That fellow North," Fred whispered. "He get Black Jack or what?"

Fulwider watched orange firelight play over the man's doughy features. "He got him," he said, after a moment.

"I knew it. Wake up, John! You owe me five!"

The deputies accompanied their charge to Rebellion, where he was confined to his hotel room for six days, allowed out only to eat. At the end of that period the posse came dragging in on hollow-flanked horses, their faces sunburned and stubbled. North wasn't with them.

An hour after he had seen them straggle past under his

window, Fulwider was summoned to the sheriff's office. There he found Oscar Adamson still in his duster, glowering from behind a big library table with a scarred blond finish that served as a desk. His hat was on the desk and the late afternoon sunlight glistened on his pink scalp where it showed through his thin gray hair. Dirty and unshaven, he looked exhausted except for his eyes.

"Kindly do not say I told you so," he grumbled.

The journalist's heart leaped, but he kept the elation from his tone. "How close did you get?"

"What difference does it make? He led us down false trails and over shallow cliffs and through mud holes up to a man's elbow on horseback. One man broke his leg and a friend I have known for fifteen years has stopped speaking to me. Your partner is more than three-quarters wolf or he would be in one of those cells by now." He jerked a thick thumb over his shoulder at the two barred enclosures, at present unoccupied.

"Perhaps you should have posted a bounty."

"The thought of a reward occurred to me," said the other, ignoring the irresistible barb. "In this mood, I am tempted still. But we found the bodies of Sam Fire Eye and Dick Lightfoot at the base of Angel's Peak, and from their condition it appears that you were telling the truth about what happened up there."

Fulwider studied him. "Does that mean North is no longer wanted?"

"I just finished wiring cancellations to my pick-up order. Not that any are needed, the way he operates."

"Then I'm free to go?"

The sheriff rumpled his hair energetically, releasing a cloud of yellow dust. " 'Go' is the most important word in that question. Go, and keep going. Since you are not wanted for anything either, I have no authority to order you out of town, but Mrs. Adamson and I would consider your loss a great gain, if you understand a foreigner's use of the language.''

"When is the next train east?" asked the other.

# FINAL NOTES

In one of those twists of fate that so delight historians, a bounty of sorts was eventually paid on the hide of Black Jack, though the amount and the circumstances could hardly have been predicted.

Months after the events described in the previous narrative, an itinerant hunter roaming the forests east of the Caribou Mountains came upon the bones of a large wolf nearly a mile below Angel's Peak. On a hunch he claimed one of the few remaining patches of black-and-gray hide, cured it and sold it for whiskey money in Rebellion. The patch, eighteen inches long and shaped somewhat like a bow tie, eventually found its way into the hands of Nelson Meredith, who displayed it on a wall in his office until his dismissal following an audit of Newcastle accounts in 1888. It disappeared for a time, resurfacing behind the bar of the Timber Queen saloon in 1905, where it was destroyed in a fire that swept through town two years later. At that point, both it and Rebellion passed from the western scene.

The anonymous drifter who had sold the piece of pelt was one of the last to benefit from the slaughter locally, for the Idaho Stockmen's Association defaulted on all its debts after the terrible winter of 1886–87 brought a howling finish to the American West's thirty-year role as beef-supplier to the world. A triple-edged sword, the disaster also prompted the investigation ordered by Newcastle's Sheffield investors that resulted in the manager's disgrace, and robbed the nearby community of its livelihood, the wolfing trade. Thus were sown the seeds of its destruction twenty years before the great fire.

R. G. Fulwider returned to New York in the spring of 1886, with his cough and a suitcase bulging with notes scribbled in the fever of his confinement in the Assiniboin Inn. He was astonished upon entering the offices of the *World* to find himself a local hero, not only because of his experiences in the wild, but also on the basis of the rumor that he had spent time in a frontier jail on a charge of gunslinging. His attempts to convince his superiors and fellow workers of both his innocence and the fact that he had spent his imprisonment in a hotel room and not behind bars proved fruitless. Joseph Pulitzer congratulated him in person upon his miraculous "escape" and promoted him to the *World*'s elite corps of troubleshooting reporters. In this capacity, his scarecrow frame was seen dangling from steam cranes over burning buildings and bobbing among crowds of police officers during raids on moonlit gambling establishments for months until someone in authority came to his senses and returned him to his rightful station behind a desk.

Fulwider died at his home in upstate New York in 1913. His age alone (69) has led physicians interested in his complaint to suggest that what his doctors diagnosed as "consumptive bronchitis" was in his case more bronchitic than consumptive. Whatever his handicap, it failed to stand in the way of a momentous career that included service as a correspondent in Cuba during the Spanish-American War, and ended with an appointment by the Governor of the

State of New York to fill out the unexpired term of a United States Senator. His plans to seek a term on his own were interrupted by his sudden death due to heart failure.

In 1902 the former journalist, besieged with requests to publish an account of the time he spent with Asa North in the mountains, engaged an operative of the Pinkerton National Detective Agency to locate the Wolfer. It was a difficult assignment, as evidenced by the agent's lengthy typewritten report submitted twelve weeks later, detailing quite as many false trails and hardships as complained of by Sheriff Adamson sixteen years earlier. Clipped to it was a travelworn letter in a woman's clear, firm hand, here reprinted.

> *Duluth, Minnesota*
> *April 11, 1902*

*Dear Mr. Powell:*

*With regret I must inform you of the death last autumn in my boardinghouse of Mr. Asa North, whom you asked about in your letter of the 2nd.*

*He was with us for two months only, and for much of that time was in a "bad way" physically, unable to eat anything more substantial than the weakest beef and inclined to regurgitate the merest scrap of meat which found its way through the sieve, with results most painful and piteous. He was visited twice by our family doctor, who following his second examination pronounced the patient to be suffering from carcinoma of the colon, a disease which he explained is incurable except by surgery, and then only in its earliest stages, after which it is always fatal. He advised me to make Mr. North's last days as comfortable as possible and said that when the time came he would make the necessary arrangements through his office.*

*Mr. North was in much pain throughout the last week. At length he fell into delirium, during which it was necessary to board my two children at the neighbor's to prevent exposing them to the foul language into which he was disposed to burst at any moment without warning. During the last three days he would eat nothing. Early on the morning of the last day the household was aroused by a long, screeching bellow issuing from his room, at which time I hastened in to find him clutching the brass bedposts behind his head in both fists, back arched, eyes wide and staring, his nostrils distened and his teeth bared in a hideous grimace. Whereupon he lapsed into a coma and did not regain consciousness. He expired at 4:08 p.m.*

*He was buried in the neighborhood churchyard, but since no one knew his birthdate (he appeared to be in his early fifties) only his name and the date of his death (October 26) were inscribed upon the stone. Both the stone and the burial were paid for out of funds in his possession at the time of his death. What remained went toward recompensing me for his care.*

*You mentioned in your letter that Mr. North had been a "wolfer," and a number of comments he let slip in his delirium would seem to confirm this, but such was not his occupation when he came to live beneath my roof as at that time he owned neither horse nor weapon.*

> *Respectfully,*
> *Nora Crain Carmichael*

At the bottom of the last page of the letter was a short note written in a flowery hand made deliberate with age.

   As I am certain that she was unaware of my existence, I never corresponded with Mrs. Carmichael. Had I done so, I would have felt obliged to explain to her that Asa North's last utterance was not, as she described it, a "bellow," but rather a howl.

# ACKNOWLEDGMENTS

The massive campaign to exterminate the Great Plains wolf is a fascinating and appalling chapter in the history of the West that has received short shrift in modern retrospectives and almost no notice at all in literature. Prompted by man's primitive hatred and fear of a fellow predator, it rivaled the wholesale slaughter that swept the bison to near-extinction, and yet few people today are even aware that it took place. Because of this the problem of obtaining research material on the subject was a towering one.

The author is grateful to a number of persons and institutions for providing him with excerpts from obscure texts and newspaper articles of the period. The former included typewritten transcriptions of eyewitness testimony volunteered by aging wolfers, many of which have never been published and might long since have gone the way of all paper but for these unsung guardians of posterity: Jim Davis, Librarian, Idaho State Historical Society, Boise; Philip J. Roberts, Research Historian, Wyoming State Archives and Historical Department, Cheyenne; Constance M. Soja, Research Assistant, Oregon Historical Society, Portland; and the staff of the Montana Historical Society, Helena.

Without their dedication and assistance *The Wolfer* would still be a maddening itch at the base of the author's occipital lobe.

For those who would seek further information on the subjects of wolf hunting and the creatures themselves, the following nonfiction works are highly recommended: *Never Cry Wolf* by Farley Mowat (Little, Brown & Co., Boston, Toronto, 1963); *The Wolf* by L. David Mech (Graphic Arts Division, the American Museum of Natural History, Garden City, New York, 1970); *Of Wolves and Men* by Barry Holstun Lopez (Charles Scribner's Sons, New York, 1978); *The Wolf in North American History* by Stanley Young (The Caxton Printers, Caldwell, Idaho, 1946); and *The Cult of the Wild* by Boyce Rensberger (Anchor Press/Doubleday, Garden City, New York, 1977), pp. 48–81.

But for the above-mentioned works, whose main focus is quite rightly on the animals rather than their pursuers, almost the only modern mention of the Great Butchery is to be found in books dealing with the wolves' brothers in disaster, the bison or American buffalo. No evening is wasted if it is spent with these excellent and highly readable histories: *The Buffalo Book* by David A. Dary (The Swallow Press, Chicago, 1974); *The Hunting of the Buffalo* by E. Douglas Branch (University of Nebraska Press, Lincoln, Nebraska, 1962); *The Buffalo* by Francis Haines (Thomas Y. Crowell Company, New York, 1975); and *The Great Buffalo Hunt* by Wayne Gard (University of Nebraska Press, Lincoln, Nebraska, 1968).

Loren D. Estleman is a prolific and versatile author who, since the publication of his first novel in 1976, has established himself as a leading writer of both mystery and Western fiction. His novels include *Mister St. John, Murdock's Law, The Glass Highway, The Midnight Man, Stamping Ground,* and the winner of the Western Writers of America's 1981 Golden Spur Award for Best Historical Western, *Aces & Eights.*

# Penguin Putnam Inc.
## Online

Your Internet gateway to a virtual environment with
hundreds of entertaining and enlightening books from
Penguin Putnam Inc.

*While you're there, get the latest buzz on
the best authors and books around—*

Tom Clancy, Patricia Cornwell, W.E.B. Griffin,
Nora Roberts, William Gibson, Robin Cook,
Brian Jacques, Catherine Coulter, Stephen King,
Jacquelyn Mitchard, and many more!

Penguin Putnam Online is located at
http://www.penguinputnam.com

# PENGUIN PUTNAM NEWS

Every month you'll get an inside look at our upcoming
books and new features on our site. This is an ongoing
effort to provide you with the most up-to-date
information about our books and authors.

Subscribe to Penguin Putnam News at
http://www.penguinputnam.com/ClubPPI